Also By R.W. Wallace

The Ghost Detective Series
Beyond the Grave
Unveiling the Past
Beneath the Surface
Piercing the Veil

Ghost Detective Short Stories
Just Desserts
Lost Friends
Family Bonds
Common Ground
Till Death
Family History
Heritage
New Beginnings
Far From Home
Severed Ties
Eternal Bond

The Tolosa Mystery Series
The Red Brick Haze
The Red Brick Cellars
The Red Brick Basilica

R.W. WALLACE
Author of the Ghost Detective Series

DEEP DARK SECRETS

A MYSTERY SHORT STORY COLLECTION

Deep Dark Secrets
by R.W. Wallace

"Hidden Horrors" Copyright © 2020 by R.W. Wallace
"Out of Sight" Copyright © 2019 by R.W. Wallace
"Cold Blue Eternity" Copyright © 2020 by R.W. Wallace
"Sitting Duck" Copyright © 2019 by R.W. Wallace
"Just Desserts" Copyright © 2020 by R.W. Wallace

Cover by the author
Cover Illustration 16661627 © James Thew | Adobe Stock

All characters and events in this book, other than those clearly in the public domain, are fictitious and any resemblance to real persons, living or dead, is purely coincidental.

All rights reserved. No part of this publication may be reproduced, distributed, or transmitted in any form or by any means, including photocopying, recording, or other electronic or mechanical methods, without the prior written permission of the publisher, except in the case of brief quotations embodied in critical reviews and certain other noncommercial uses permitted by copyright law.

www.rwwallace.com
Varden Publishing
Unit 95090, PO Box 6945, London, W1A 6US

ISBN paperback: [979-10-95707-67-7]
ISBN ebook: [979-10-95707-68-4]

First Edition

TABLE OF CONTENTS

Introduction	1
Hidden Horrors	**3**
Out of Sight	27
Cold Blue Eternity	**47**
Sitting Duck	**81**
Just Desserts	**101**
Author's Note	134
Also by R.W. Wallace	135

INTRODUCTION

I HAVE PUSBLISHED almost all my short stories as standalones. The reason for this is not to get all the money, because individual short stories don't sell all that well (except that one young adult one, I have yet to understand what happened there), but to gain experience in publishing books. There are so many things to learn, and so many possible pitfalls (like when I had two chapters 5 and no chapter 7, and let's not forget the chapter with two random pages missing—I caught both before they went into the world!). A second motivation, and this one is actually quite important: I love holding the book in my hand, even when it's not much more than a leaflet for a 6000-word short story.

I did, however, have the grand plan to publish collections once I had enough stories to fill them. Except I never got around to it. Until I signed up for a publishing challenge (publish one book per month for a year) and started scouring my backlist to see what I could come up with. Well, over twenty short stories, for one.

Now, how to group them into collections that make sense?

Having a predilection for mystery, I quickly rounded up the stories to fill two collections. Started doing the layout, the cover... only to discover I had no idea what the title should be. Or the theme. Or...

Oh, wait, there *is* a logic to all this! When going through the five stories, I suddenly saw a pattern. Sort of.

They're all about secrets. Dark ones. Deep ones. Secrets that shape us and the people and world around us.

So there's your theme, and your title. And isn't the cover fun?

Now I invite you to kick back with these short tales, some taking place in France, some in Norway, and one with a bit of a fantasical element.

Enjoy!

R.W. Wallace
www.rwwallace.com

HIDDEN HORRORS

ONE

Take a deep breath in through the nose. Out through the mouth.

I inhale deeply. The smell of figs reach me through the open window, even though the compost is at the far end of the garden. My husband Marc spent the afternoon raking below the fig tree and the smell of ripe fruit is going to be an integral part of our back yard for a while.

My pantry is filling up with pots of jam. When I reached twenty pots, I decided we had enough to last our family of four until next year. The last batch of figs went into a pie, and the rest I hereby offer to the blackbirds and the wasps.

On the next breath, gently close your eyes and let your breathing go back to normal.

Dammit, my mind wandered again. I follow the instructions and let my eyes close.

Open your senses. Feel your contact with your surroundings. Sounds. Smells.

Well, my ass is firmly planted on my chair and I'm feeling nice and heavy. The murmur of the cars from the highway is fairly faint today, like it always is on a heavy and humid summer night. The neighbors are having a party again, but it's not too noisy. Just some chatting between friends and some low-key music. Madame Humbert next door keeps complaining about them every time we meet. She apparently feels that owning a house in a somewhat rich neighborhood should protect you against anyone below the age of twenty-five. Too bad the neighbor decided he'd rent out his house to a group of five students.

A gentle smile touches my lips. I happen to like the youngsters. Makes the backyard feel alive and fun. Almost magical in its calmness.

Now bring your focus to your breath.

Aaaah! Meditation. I'm meditating, not judging my neighbors. I'm never going to get the hang of this.

I focus on my breath. I know how to do this. Chest rising, stomach growing. Chest lowering, stomach back in. Rinse and repeat.

The guy on the meditation app doesn't always say the same thing, but a couple of sessions ago, he mentioned imagining swinging back and forth in your mind. It certainly helped me staying focused on the breath and not go off on tangents every thirty seconds.

So I imagine myself on a swing. I breathe in and I swing forward. I breathe out and I swing backward. I feel the wind in my hair, log brown strands flapping in my eyes on the return. I'm wearing a pink sun dress—I think it's my favorite from when I was five years old.

In my mind, I'm five-year-old me, swinging from the branches of the apple tree in my parents' garden, smiling from ear to ear.

I can see the butterflies, feel the sun on my face. Hear my mother calling in the background.

I tighten my hold on the ropes and lean back so I'm horizontal on the forward swing. More wind. Going higher.

Smiling wider.

This feels so good. Gone is the stress from work. I'm not wondering if my daughter has done her homework. I'm not feeling guilty about not having cleaned the downstairs bathroom like I'd planned. My only goal is to go higher, faster.

At the top of my curve, as I start to breathe out, I'm weightless. My dress floats around me and I'm frozen in space for just a second.

Then I breathe out and I swing back.

Next breath in, and I lean into it again. This time, when I reach the top, it feels like the swing is holding me back.

What happens if I let go?

I continue my meditation, breathing in and out, leaning into the swing on every breath in. *Can* I let go? Could that be the point of the meditation? To just let everything go?

The guy on the app talks, something about not worrying if the mind wanders, but I'm tuning him out. I keep swinging, keep reliving details from my childhood.

I hear my mother's voice again. She's telling me she's going to take a shower.

I haven't heard her voice in over thirty years. In fact, I can't quite remember the very last time I heard it, though I know I was five. One thing I do remember is fighting with my dad because I wanted to wear the pink sun dress to the funeral, but he wouldn't let me.

I'm still leaning into every swing and my butt is leaving the swing at the top of every curve. Only my hands on the ropes are holding me back.

I used to love jumping off the swing at top speed.

When did I stop doing that?

I decide *to hell with it*. On the next breath in, I lean into the swing with all my might. But instead of holding on at the top—I let go.

I'm flying.

Pink dress around my ears. Feet toward the sky. Arms flailing.

I land with a *thump*.

God, this feels real. I've lost all contact with my body sitting in a chair in my bedroom at home. All I can feel is the need to *breathe*. Where did all the air go?

I roll over on my side and realize I'm lying in the grass. Some ten meters away I see the old swing moving lazily back and forth now that I'm no longer there to boost it, sunlight dappling the wooden seat as it shines through the leaves of the apple tree.

I still can't draw breath. My brain knows it'll come back eventually, but my body's still panicking.

I remember this. It's not a memory I ever think about, but this really happened. I was wearing my pretty dress and wanted to watch it as I flew through the air. But I miscalculated and let go too late, so I didn't manage to land on my feet.

Finally, I manage to draw a breath.

Then push it right back out in an ear-splitting scream.

My arm's hurting. Now that my lungs are working again, the rest of my body's letting itself be known.

Though I'm feeling the pain and the panic of my little body, I'm also observing as an adult. I'm watching five-year-old me crying and screaming for her mother because she's in pain and she's scared.

I miss knowing that I have someone who'll always come when I call for help.

Mom doesn't disappoint. Seconds after my scream, she comes hurtling out the kitchen door, wearing nothing but a pair of white panties and a pink bra. She must have been on her way into the shower.

She sprints across the lawn and kneels at my side, putting her hands on both sides of my face. "Where does it hurt, honey? What happened?"

I realize I'm still screaming. Mom manages to get her questions in when I draw breath. I will myself to stop, but I have no power over what's going on. I'm only along for the ride as a passenger.

I'm somehow reliving a memory from my childhood that I'd completely forgotten about. But now that I see it, I know it really happened. I know traumatic incidents can cause memory loss, but a broken arm doesn't feel like it should be traumatic enough.

"I don't think it's broken, honey," Mom says. She's figured out it's the arm that's the problem and has gently rolled me to the side so she can inspect it. "Maybe sprained something, but there's no blood. Can you move your fingers for me?"

I'm still screaming, but by shorter bouts, and with less volume. It seems like the thing to do when you're suffering.

I move my fingers and Mom rewards me with a huge smile.

"See? Not broken." She caresses my cheek with one hand. "But I realize it's hurting, honey. Do you think you can walk up to the house? I just need to get dressed, then we'll go to see the doctor so he can heal it."

But five-year-old me doesn't think I can get up. Even the idea of moving around is making me go back to the original blood-curdling screams.

"Don't cry, baby," Mom coos. "I'll carry you in."

"Do you need any help, Ma'am?" a male voice says from the street.

My mother freezes and glances down at her mostly naked body. There's a hedge separating our garden from the street, but it's not very high—well, it is for five-year-old me, but not for adults—and anyone can just step through.

Five year-old me doesn't think much about my mother looking down at herself, except to note that her bra is the exact same beautiful pink as my dress, but adult me cringes at finding yourself half naked in front of a stranger. Depending on the person on the other side of the hedge, they could even sue for public indecency if they were so inclined.

Mom's chest is heaving rapidly and her face is very pale. My continued screaming probably isn't helping. Clenching her teeth together, she raises her head to face the stranger. "My daughter fell and hurt her arm," she says calmly.

"Can I be of assistance?" I can't see the man since my eyes are focused solely on Mom, but his voice is calm and polite. At least it doesn't sound like he'll go after her for walking around in plain view in her underwear.

Mom hesitates. But I'd always been on the big side and she'd been refusing to carry me for over a year already. With a broken or sprained arm to boot, it was mission impossible.

"Would you mind helping me carry her to the house?" she asks.

"Of course." I hear the rustling of someone pushing through the hedge and then he comes to stand in my field of vision, right behind my mother. He has dark blond hair, brown eyes, and a nose that's too small for his face. His lips are a little on the thin side, but they lift into a smile as he looks at me.

Then the smile turns decidedly lecherous as he lets his eyes wander down my mother's back while she has her back turned.

Five-year-old me only thinks he must be admiring the pretty pink like I did, but adult me has a cold finger running down my spine. I want to tell her to make the man go away, to tell him she'll manage on her own.

I prefer to see the old one with my own eyes before giving an estimate."

We reach the kitchen and Mom points to one of the chairs. "Would you mind setting her down there, please?"

George deposits me on the chair and I throw my arms around Mom—including the hurt one, proving it isn't all that hurt—and downgrade the screams to hulks.

As Mom whispers reassurances into my ear, I watch George watching us. Ankles crossed, he leans against the kitchen counter as he leisurely admires my mother's behind again. He glances at his watch, then back to my mother's body, then out the window, where he has a panoramic view of our entire street.

"You'll be fine, honey," my mother tells me as she rubs my back. "Mom just needs to go get dressed, all right? Can you stay here with the nice man for one minute while I go get some pants and a t-shirt?"

Adult me heaves a relieved breath as five-year-old me hold on tighter around Mom's neck.

How can I not know what's going to happen? As the events run their course, the memories resurface. I *know* this actually happened. But I have no idea what's going to happen in a second, or in a minute, or in an hour.

And I don't like it. Any of it. Fear is burning in my stomach and I'm unable to tell which version of me is doing that.

Perhaps it's both.

George pushes away from the counter and comes to stand next to my mother. Adult me figures this gives him a perfect view of her cleavage.

He brushes a hand through my hair. "Don't worry, kiddo. We'll be fine for a minute, won't we?"

Mom's gaze zeroes in on his hand. The tiniest of lines appears between her eyebrows. "Actually," she says, her voice falsely light, "I can get dressed after we take care of the arm."

She forces my arms off her neck, making my hulks go back to screams, and gets up to face George. "Thank you so much for your help, George. I can take it from here." When he makes no move to leave, she adds, "Perhaps you'd like to leave through the front door, so you don't need to go through the hedge again?"

George lets his gaze run slowly from my mother's head to her toes. "Actually," he says and lifts a hand to run along one of her bra's pink straps. "I think I'd like to stay a little longer. You don't resist and I promise not to touch the kid."

TWO

I NEVER KNEW the details around my mother's death. I knew she'd been murdered and I knew they'd never found the killer.

The first times I'd asked my father, he'd say I was too young. He kept the information from me to protect me.

As I grew older, I realized that me asking the question hurt *him*. Made him even more distant. So I stopped asking. I cherished the memories I had of Mom and came to terms with the fact that my mother was a cold case.

A couple of times, the police came to talk to my dad. The last time was when I was twenty-eight and home on vacation, and this time I was considered adult enough to listen in. They'd discovered some new method for doing DNA tests and wanted Dad's authorization to do new checks on the little evidence they'd gathered at the murder scene.

They actually had the DNA. That wasn't the problem. The problem was that the killer wasn't in any of the databases.

Still, Dad always agreed to let them reopen the case. Before going back to staring at the wall.

Even then, once the police had left, I didn't ask my dad about the circumstances of Mom's death. I figured the reason he didn't want to give me the details was that he didn't know them himself.

I never realized it was because I *did* know them.

༅

THERE'S BLOOD *EVERYWHERE*.

The kitchen's covered in it. I'm not really taking in any other details, though. I understand why I suppressed these memories, why I can't remember my Mom's last words. It's just too horrific.

I'm still screaming. This time, I'm in complete agreement with my five-year-old self, and help her along to keep screaming, even when the voice is gone and it can't really qualify for anything but hissing.

She never closes her eyes, so I see everything.

When it's all over, George stands above me, panting. His clothes are covered in my mother's blood.

I look up at him, wondering what he'll do. I don't remember it—I still only remember things as they happen—but I'm not actually afraid he'll hurt me. I'm still alive, aren't I?

It gives me the calmness I need to continue observing. Five-year-old me isn't so lucky.

"Time to stop screaming, kid," he says. He sits down on his haunches to come face to face with me. His hair is covered in blood, his chin has a deep gouge—this is where the DNA they found under Mom's fingernails would have come from—and his pupils are so dilated I can barely make out the brown of the iris.

"Stop screaming or I'll hurt you."

The screaming stops. Hiccups start up instead, but George doesn't seem to mind.

"You're not going to tell anyone about this, are you?" His eyelids are heavy as he studies me. He oozes confidence, as if he's not worried in the least of getting caught.

I expect my head to start shaking, but nothing happens. Just another hiccup.

"What's your name, kiddo?" he asks.

No reply.

"Give me a nod and I'll let you go to your room."

Still nothing.

One side of his thin lips lift in a satisfied smile and he slaps his hands on his bloody knees, pushing off to get back up.

I just sit there and watch as he gets ready to leave. He takes his time about it, too. He goes to the bathroom to take a shower. He takes a plastic bag and shoves all his dirty clothes inside. He left the door open, so I can see him from my spot in the kitchen. He has a birthmark on the back of his upper thigh—it's three overlapping circles and they make me think of Mickey Mouse.

He goes to my parents' room and I hear him rummaging around in the closet. Five minutes later, he emerges wearing one of my Dad's suits. It's a bit short in the legs, but it's not obvious he's wearing another man's clothes.

He grabs the plastic bag, and without so much as a backward glance at me or my mother, throws out a carefree, "Later, kiddo," before slamming the kitchen door shut behind him. I see him jumping the hedge at the back of the garden, leading to a small wood that I'd never been to because my parents judged it too dangerous.

༄

I SIT THERE, in my five-year-old body, for what feels like an eternity. How long is this trip down memory lane supposed to last? Until I catch up to the next thing I actually remember? That's probably the fight about the dress for the funeral, which will be *days* away.

God, I hope I won't be stuck here for that long.

Dong.

I slam back into my adult body.

What's going on?

Dong.

It's the bloody meditation app. My twenty minutes of meditation are up, and it always ends on three gongs. I never understood what those were for, but now I'm wondering if it's in order to bring lost souls back to their bodies when the time is right.

I'm still sitting in my chair, facing the window. The figs are stinking up the garden. The blackbirds are singing, and the cars are humming.

My body is covered in sweat and I'm shaking. My throat feels raw. I try to say a few words, but they come out hoarse and rusty.

Feet shaking, I stand up just as the doorbell rings.

Feeling completely lost, I make it down to open the door. It's Mathilda from next door.

"Is everything all right?" she asks. "I heard screaming."

I lift a hand to my throat. "Sorry about that. I fell asleep. Bad dream."

Mathilda doesn't seem entirely convinced, but we're not really close enough for her to pry. "All right," she says. She points a finger at me. "But you come tell me if you need anything, you hear?"

I nod. "Will do, Mathilda. Thank you."

I close the front door, then just stand there looking at it for several minutes.

THREE

I'M BACK IN my hometown. I told my husband I had to help out a friend, so he would take the kids after school, and just drove for three hours to get there.

I'm not in front of our old house, though. I'm on the other side of town, in a neighborhood that's very similar, except it has fences instead of hedges. The house I'm staring at is identical to all the other houses on this street, with beige plaster, white windows, and blue shutters. The mailbox is on the original side, probably homemade, and sports the name George Lambert.

My phone is in my hand, with my Dad's face staring up at me. My thumb is hovering above the call button.

Before I can decide to hit send, a car drives up behind me, and the automatic gate starts to slide open. I turn to see a white Opel idling on the street, waiting to drive into its garage.

The driver is a man in his fifties. Dark blond hair. Difficult to judge when he's sitting in his car, but he seems tall.

He turns to look at me, and I freeze as I recognize him. Same too-small nose. Same thin lips.

The passenger window lowers. "Can I help you with anything, Ma'am?"

I'm frozen in place, but after a couple of seconds I manage a tight shake of my head. My thumb is still ready to press send, though the screen has gone black.

"Well," the man—George—says. "That's my house you're staring at. If you don't have any business with me, I'd appreciate it if you'd move along."

My pulse is beating about a thousand thumps a minute and a drop of sweat trickles down between my breasts despite the cooling evening air.

"Bathroom," I blurt out.

"What?" George had started accelerating to drive his car into the garage, but the car stops after ten centimeters. He seems to study me closer, giving me a quick once-over. "I don't do bathrooms anymore," he says slowly. "Moved over to kitchens over twenty years ago."

He cocks his head and narrows his eyes. "Do I know you from somewhere, lady?"

I shake my head. I'm finally able to get my hands to work and I unlock my phone and press dial.

A car honks its horn behind me. Someone from farther down the street getting impatient with George blocking his way.

With an irritated glance behind him, George drives his Opel into the garage.

"Hey, honey," Dad says. "What's up?"

My body's frozen in place, but my voice still works. "I found him, Dad," I say. "His name is George Lambert."

Dad talks back to me, but I don't hear him. George is coming out of the garage and my first reflex is to drop my phone into my purse.

George stalks through the still-open gate and straight up to me. His face is exactly the same as I saw in my memory mere hours ago, except he's aged thirty years. A little bit of a beer gut. Less hair. But still the man who murdered my mother right in front of my eyes.

"Are you sure we've never met?" he asks. "You look familiar."

I shake my head again. "I'm sorry to have bothered you, Sir. I was just going for a walk and stopped here to check something on my phone."

His gaze never leaves my face. He chews on his lower lip as he studies me and I can practically see the gears turning in his head.

His eyes harden and his lips curl into a smirk. "You wouldn't happen to have owned a pink sun dress when you were about five?"

I can't help it; I gulp as I stare into his brown eyes. "I don't—"

"Anne, wasn't it?" He gives me a once-over, and I can't hold back the shiver that takes me over as I remember him giving my mother the exact same look. "I don't think I had the honor of learning your name face to face, but the papers were more than helpful in filling in some details."

He stares into my eyes, and although he's twenty years my senior, I'm all too aware of the fact that he's a good head taller than me. "What brings you to my door?" he asks.

"I don't know what you're—"

He grabs my elbow and steers me through the gate and toward his front door. "Why don't you come in for a cup of coffee? I believe we have some catching up to do." With one firm hand on my elbow, he uses the other to fish his keys out of his pocket while he looks up and down the street. His gaze lingers for a moment on a house a little farther down the street—the house of the man honking his horn earlier, if I wasn't mistaken.

As he opens the door, I try to break free, but he must have seen it coming. In a gesture that would probably look friendly from afar, he grabs my shoulders and pulls me inside.

Locking the door and putting the keys back in his pocket, he uses his body to force me up against the door. "How did you find me?"

My voice is shaking. "Google."

He rolls his eyes. "How did you know who to look for?"

"I saw you," I whisper.

"Of course you did." He looks like he wants to do another eye-roll but stops himself. "So after thirty years, you thought it would be time to look me up?"

My breathing is shallow and my heart threatens to jump out of my chest. "I'd like to leave now."

"Sorry," George says casually. "No can do."

He grabs the front of my shirt and pulls me behind him down a hallway.

I try to fight him, but he's so much stronger than him, I feel like I'm back in my five-year-old body.

He opens a door, and unceremoniously throws me through it.

It takes longer than expected to hit the floor—because it's not a floor, but a staircase. I tumble down, hitting my head and my hips and breaking two fingers on my left hand. At the bottom, I heave for breath and cradle my hand against my chest.

George comes down the staircase, taking his time. "Now, I'd love to do this in the kitchen," he says. "For old times' sake. But unfortunately, I'll need to clean up my mess this time, and down here is just going to be that much more practical."

Since I woke up from my meditation, I have been working mostly in a state of shock. On seeing George, I added a good dose of fear. Tumbling down the stairs, pain.

Now, as I see my mother's murderer come toward me while he rolls up the sleeves of his shirt, anger is finally making its entry.

This man destroyed my family. Ruined my childhood. Made my father into a zombie who hardly ever shakes out of his funk for long enough to come visit his grandchildren.

I am not going down without a fight.

George might think he was up against a second version of my mother. I certainly look like her. And while, physically, that might be true, there is a very important difference between today and that fateful day thirty years ago.

I don't have a child to worry about in addition to my own safety. And I know what to expect.

George talks as he takes his time on the stairs, explaining all the horrors he's going to do to me. I tune him out, having heard him say much the same things to my mother only hours earlier. Instead, I look around, searching for anything that could help me.

○3

Though I hate how vulnerable it will make me, I let George start his show without fighting back. It was what my mother had done, so I assume he won't find it surprising. When he approaches, I walk backwards until my back hits the counter of a workbench, then freeze.

He seems to want a repeat of my mother's murder—where the first order on the agenda is to remove my clothes. In my mother's case, that had meant ripping off her underwear, but for me, he'd have a little more work. He grabs my blouse at the neck and rips it open, exposing my chest to the chill cellar air.

He seems happy with what he sees and bends down to open my belt.

My mother had assumed he only had rape in mind when he started, not murder. And she had me to look out for. So she'd let him do whatever he wanted. When she realized how far he'd go, it was too late.

I know where this is going from the start, and my kids are safe with their father hundreds of kilometers away.

I lean back and stretch my hand toward the rack above the workbench. I grab whatever I touch first and barely have the time to register that it's a huge wrench before slamming it down on George's head.

He crumples at my feet, blood oozing from a wound just above his ear.

I don't even bother to check if he's breathing, I just run for the stairs.

The door's locked. I try to force it open, but I don't have the necessary body weight. Just as I consider the possibility of going back down to look for my purse—which I must have lost at some point during my fall down the stairs—I hear sirens.

༺

I sit in the back of an ambulance, letting medical personnel look after my broken fingers, when they bring George out of the house. The left half of his face is covered in blood, but he's walking on his own and his eyes are locked on mine for the entire walk between his front door and the waiting police car.

With my uninjured right hand, I hold my phone to my ear and listen to my father's voice. He'd kept the connected call on his cell phone while using the land line to call the police. Somehow, he'd understood that something very bad was happening and sent the police after the name I gave him.

"How long have you known?" he asks me. His voice is shaky.

"Just a few hours, Dad," I reply. "I only discovered the memory this afternoon."

He's silent for a moment. "Everything?"

I close my eyes. "Yes. But he'll be going to prison now. Mom will finally get justice."

We sit in silence, enjoying the cool evening in two different cities.

"Maybe I could come visit this weekend," Dad says. "I haven't seen the kids in a while."

"That'd be great, Dad."

OUT OF SIGHT

ONE

Gérard Blanc walked through the door at five to seven, while Christine Blanc sat curled up in the corner of the couch, reading a mystery novel. She'd sat there for exactly twenty minutes, grabbing her daily dose of time for herself.

The house was tidy and clean, the fridge was full of groceries, her son had finished his homework and was currently drowning himself in music in his room, and the trash cans were already on the sidewalk, ready for tomorrow morning. She deserved some time-out with a funny detective and gritty murders.

Tomorrow she'd be back at work, with everyone asking her how her "second weekend" had been. Always said with a wink and a laugh, because everybody knew that the moms taking Wednesdays off didn't do it to slack off, but it hurt—just a little—nonetheless. Her son Louis might be fifteen, so he didn't exactly need her to take him to the park anymore—though she did drive him to soccer practice in the afternoon—but there was still a ton of stuff to do. And since she had this day off every week, everybody—with her husband Gérard first in line—assumed this meant all household tasks fell to her.

Need to go to the bank? Christine can do it on Wednesday. Louis needs new clothes? Christine can do it on Wednesday. Laundry? Cut the grass? Dentist's appointment for Louis? Wednesday.

She didn't mind doing the work. Really. She loved being useful to her family and enjoying a pretty home. There were just some...details...yet to be worked out for everything to run smoothly.

"Ah, you vacuumed, I see," Gérard said as he spotted the vacuum in the middle of the living room. "Excellent." He removed his leather shoes, placed them in the shoe rack by the door, deposited his bag in its usual spot in the closet, and approached his wife with a genuine smile.

He leaned over the back of the couch and gave her a kiss on the top of her head. "Did you have a good day?" His scruff caught in Christine's hair and she caught a faint whiff of his deodorant mixed with sweat. It had been a sweltering hot day. Apparently even the air-conditioning in the office wasn't enough when wearing a suit and tie.

Christine closed her book and returned her husband's smile. "Yes, thank you," she replied. "I'll just put away the vacuum, and dinner will be ready in five minutes. Would you mind telling Louis to come down?"

Gérard cocked his head in direction of their son's room as he removed his tie. "He's going to go deaf if he continues like that."

Christine shrugged.

"I guess he had to turn into a real teenager at some point." Gérard hung his jacket in the closet before taking the steps two at a time. "Louis! Dinner in five."

Christine had to force her frown away. Louis *had* changed in the last couple of months. He always listened to his music, didn't come down to talk to her when he'd finished his homework, hardly ever smiled.

Somehow, she'd thought she'd gotten the perfect boy. Who wouldn't rebel and stay her little darling.

The music blared even louder, meaning Gérard opened Louis's door. Christine winced. She wouldn't say anything.

It wouldn't help.

ɞ

As CHRISTINE WALKED through the front door, she was hit first by a blast of the welcome fresh air of a house where the stores had been closed all day, then by a deafening wall of angry music.

Closing the door behind her, Christine stood still in the hallway for several moments, staring at the stairwell leading to her son's room.

The house looked so quiet. Stores down, uncluttered tables. Everything still.

But that *noise*.

She didn't even know what type of music it was. Perhaps *Rage Against the Machine*? The name certainly fit. It most certainly was *not* the rock and old French ballads he used to listen to. How she missed Georges Brassens.

With a deep breath, Christine pushed aside the lingering stress from work, took off her shoes, and went up the stairs.

She knocked on his door and waited a few seconds even though there was no way he could hear her.

"Louis?" she yelled as she opened the door. "You have to turn the music down!"

The room was pitch black. Blinds down and curtains drawn. Even the digital alarm clock was absent. He must have unplugged it.

Head pounding because of the noise, Christine flicked on the light and made a beeline for the stereo. Guessing the music was actually coming from Louis's phone, she pulled the plug.

Blessed silence. And ringing ears.

She wanted to yell at him. For ruining his hearing. For bothering the neighbors.

She didn't.

"Louis?" she said, her voice soft. "What's going on?"

The comforter moved on the bed, Louis completely covered and curling into a ball. "Go away. I'm sleeping."

Christine stared at the comforter, not daring to go sit next to him. "Did you do your homework?"

"Go away."

Christine considered opening the stores but decided she didn't need to antagonize him even further. She looked around the room, at a loss.

On the desk in the corner, usually covered in books and homework, a large, hairy ball.

Christine sucked in a breath and recoiled. Then she recognized it.

"You cut your hair?" In two strides she was at the desk, delving her hand into locks of curly blond hair. Gérard's electric razor was still plugged into the socket next to the desk, its little green light blinking as it charged its long-dead battery.

This time she went to the bed. She sat down next to the bundle that was her son and pulled at the comforter.

He'd shorn almost all his hair off. There couldn't be more than a centimeter left, leaving his scalp visible for the first time since he was two.

Christine put her hand on her son's head, needing the physical confirmation that the golden locks were gone.

Louis pushed her off the bed and disappeared back under the comforter. "I said, go away!"

Christine picked herself off the floor. She smoothed down her skirt. "Dinner will be ready in twenty minutes." Her voice was shaking.

"Not hungry. Go away."

She stood there, looking around at her son's room, wondering where her little boy had gone.

"How was Automation class today?" He'd been so enthusiastic about that class at the beginning of the school year.

"GO AWAY!"

TWO

WEDNESDAY NIGHT, AND Christine was once again enjoying her twenty minutes of mystery reading.

Louis hadn't said a word to her in over a week that wasn't some version of "Go away," but she'd managed to lower the volume of the music. She'd gone into his room one afternoon while he was hiding/sleeping under the covers and lowered the volume to something that wouldn't maim her son and wouldn't bother the neighbors. He hadn't touched the volume button since.

But the angry music continued.

Five minutes to seven, and Gérard walked through the front door. He looked around while he undid his shoelaces and put away his shoes. "What have you been up to today?"

Christine shrugged as she put her book away. "The usual." Laundry, dishes, cleaning the bathroom, picking up a package at the post office, weeding the flower garden, checking that the well was dry for the fifth year running, bringing Louis to soccer practice, paying a couple of bills, cleaning all the ground floor windows.

"Hmm," Gérard said and sat down in front of the computer. A news site was open thirty seconds later.

"Dinner will be ready in five minutes," Christine said.

༄

"Does he just not eat anymore?" Gérard put his dirty plate in the dishwasher before grabbing a yogurt from the fridge.

"I'll take a plate up to his room." Christine piled Louis's plate with spaghetti carbonara—Louis's favorite.

"You'll just encourage him to keep up his shenanigans. If he can't come down to eat with us, he can go hungry."

Christine took the food up to her son's room. "I'll just put this here," she said, loud enough to be heard over the music. "It'll do you good to eat something. Do you need anything else?"

"Go away," Louis said from the comforter.

He wasn't screaming it anymore—Christine took that for an improvement.

Back downstairs, Gérard had changed into his working-around-the-house clothes and was cleaning the living room windows.

"What are you doing?" Christine asked, voice impressively calm.

"What does it look like? I'm cleaning the windows. You can hardly see anything through them when the sun hits in the morning."

Christine closed her eyes for a moment and took a deep breath. "I know. That's why I cleaned them this afternoon. You're cleaning clean windows."

Gérard looked around the living room, apparently really looking for the first time. "Oh. Well. Right. What about upstairs?"

Waving toward the stairs, Christine replied, "You can go clean the windows upstairs."

Should she have left the cleaning stuff out so that he'd see that she'd done it? Left the clean clothes folded on the bed? Placed Louis's soccer shoes in plain view?

If he didn't see proof, it didn't happen.

Christine attacked the dishes.

༄

A WEEK LATER, Christine allowed herself an afternoon with her friend Florence, getting a much-needed break. They were at their favorite *salon de thé*, enjoying the shade, a cup of tea, and a slice of raspberry and pistachio pie.

"I'm telling you," Christine said after taking a sip of her tea. "He still goes to school and soccer practice, but other than that, he hasn't left his room in two weeks."

Florence licked her spoon to make sure there wasn't the smallest little crumb left. "Have you asked him what the problem is?"

"Of course I have. He just tells me to go away." Christine sighed. "I guess we're just starting in on the dreaded teenage years."

pull him out. Then she got carried away, and now everything's snowballing."

"Louis certainly never has anything but praise for the man," Christine agreed. "By the way, did you hear that Dorian's mom—ah, I never remember her name, it's something really short—has quit her job?"

"Oh!" Florence's eyes lit with glee. "I did hear. But my sources have it she was fired. She's just saying she quit to save face."

Chuckling, Christine leaned back in her chair. "Do tell."

ௐ

"How did that go?" Christine set the casserole on the trivet and took her seat.

"They asked if we'd seen anything on the Wednesday he'd gone missing. Also where we'd been. Hah! As if one of the parents would take off with the Automation teacher!"

"Quite."

"Anyway, I told them I'd been at work and that you'd been busy all day. I remember it quite clearly. You'd been really busy that Wednesday. Vacuuming, laundry, gardening. That's the day you turned the well into a compost!"

Christine filled her husband's plate, then her own. "Was it? I can hardly tell one Wednesday from the next."

"Oh, yes. I remember. You'd had so much to do, it wasn't even all done when I got home. Vacuum out, clothes on the bed, gardening tools by the door." He gave Christine a big, bright smile. "I don't know how you do it all."

Christine smiled back at her husband. "You'd be surprised what a mother can do once she sets her mind to it."

THREE

That night—after she'd had dinner with Gérard, after bringing a plate of food to Louis's room, after the dishes—Christine decided to follow her friend's advice. She knocked on Louis's door, waited five seconds, then entered.

He'd eaten some of the food. All the pasta was gone, and a little more than half of his steak was cooling on the plate by the door.

Christine moved the plate next to the staircase, then went back to her son's room and closed the door behind her, plunging them into complete darkness.

"So how was your day?" she asked as she carefully crossed the room, moving each foot slowly in front of the other, praying she wouldn't step on anything pointy. "Did you have fun at school?"

"Go away."

"How are your friends? I haven't seen any of them around lately. Are you still hanging out?"

The sound of Gérard slamming a window shut somewhere in the house.

"Will you please talk to me, Louis? What's wrong?"

"Go away."

Christine lay down on the bed next to her son, snuggling up close to his back. "Sorry, kiddo. No can do. It's my house."

"It's my room."

"True." She put a hand on his back and started moving it in small circles, like he'd loved her to do when he was little. "How do you manage to breathe in there?"

A sigh. "Opening on the other side."

"Ah. That's one less thing for me to worry about, I guess."

Silence.

"You worry about me breathing under my comforter?"

"Of course I do. I'm your mother. Sometimes, when my mind starts playing tricks on me, I come check on you at night to make sure you're still breathing."

"That's creepy, *Maman*."

"Okay." Christine continued her caresses, and little by little, she pulled the comforter down so Louis's head was exposed. She ran her hand over his head, feeling like she was touching a soft cushion. "Your head's oddly soft when your hair's that short," she said. "Makes me want to lie here and run my hand over it all night."

Louis's voice was a whisper. "'kay."

Encouraged, Christine tried again. "How are things at school, Louis?"

A sound that might have been a sigh, might have been a sob. Or a mix of the two. "Not great."

"Is it your friends?"

"No."

"Classes? You know we won't be mad if you get bad grades, right?"

"Grades are fine."

Christine paused. Her heart beat faster in her chest and her breath shortened.

"Teachers?" she asked.

"Teacher."

ෆ

THE REASON SO many French moms took Wednesdays off was that there was no school on Wednesday afternoon. It meant they had the morning to take care of the house, the garden, rendez-vous, and shopping, then spent the afternoon either playing with their young kids or driving the not so young ones to various sports and activities.

Teachers also had Wednesday afternoons off.

"Monsieur Georges!" Christine called as she strode out from behind the bush she'd been hiding behind for ten minutes. She had a perfect view of the teachers' entrance to the school but needed to be alert so her target didn't get away before she caught up with him.

"How lucky that I ran into you here," she said with a big smile.

home for lunch, then bring him to and from soccer practice for her. "So it's the perfect opportunity for us to get acquainted!"

The look on Monsieur George's face was priceless. You'd think the man had never been face to face with a determined mother before. He let himself be led by the elbow, though. "I don't really—"

"I have the perfect dish waiting in the oven at home. It was originally a Moroccan recipe. Pie with lamb, ginger, chickpeas, you get the idea. I'm not a big fan of lamb myself, so I've changed it to pork—which means the recipe isn't all that Moroccan anymore. But it's still delicious! And I absolutely insist that you come home and help me eat it, since Louis left me all alone."

"I was going to—"

Christine squeezed his elbow as she peered up at him. "You don't have a wife waiting for you at home, do you?"

"No, but—"

"Then it's settled! You're eating my spicy Moroccan dish and you can tell me all about how you manage to inspire your students. I'm thoroughly impressed!"

Five minutes and endless chatter later, they reached Christine's home. She shoved the teacher ahead of her and had him sit down at the kitchen table.

"Beautiful house you have here, Madame Blanc," he said. "And your garden's gorgeous." He seemed to have accepted his fate for the afternoon.

Christine still locked the front door and hid the key in a drawer.

"Thank you," she said as she pulled her pie from the oven. "It's a lot of work, but the result makes it worth it. Like having kids, I guess."

He pointed to the back of the yard. "Is that a well?"

"Used to be. It was already dry when we bought the house five years ago, and the sellers told us they'd never seen any water down there in ten years. It's very pretty though, with that wooden lid and the little contraption on top."

Christine cut the pie carefully, making six slices, and sliding one piece onto Monsieur George's place and one from the opposite side of the pie onto hers. "I'm thinking of using the well as a compost dump, actually."

Monsieur George hesitated as he squinted at the well. "How would you get the dirt out afterward?"

"Oh." Christine waved a hand. "I wouldn't. Just figured it would be prettier than that heap I have against the fence back there." She pointed to the far corner of the garden, where she'd created a large heap of grass, branches, and leaves over the years. It was the one ugly spot in her garden, which she otherwise absolutely adored since it was walled in by bushes on all sides, making it her own private little haven.

Monsieur George sniffed the plate in front of him. "This smells delicious."

"Why, thank you!" Christine grabbed a bottle of red she'd opened before leaving for school. "Here, have some wine. It's quite strong and goes perfectly with this dish."

"I really shouldn't…"

Christine filled his glass, then filled her own with water. "*Bon appétit!*"

ଓଃ

"Ah, you've vacuumed. Excellent." Gérard smiled at his wife and gave her a kiss on the top of her head.

"Yes," Christine replied. "Let me just put the vacuum away and dinner will be ready in five minutes."

Gérard stayed by the couch, his head cocked. "No music today?"

Christine smiled, genuinely this time. "He's out with his friends. Going to the movies, I think."

"Did he finish his homework?"

Rolling her eyes inside the closet as she put the vacuum away, Christine replied, "It's the last week of school, Gérard. There's no homework."

"Right. By the way, I had lunch with Cédric today."

Christine started setting the table. "Léna's dad?"

"Yes." Gérard set out two glasses and the trivet. "Did you know one of the teachers has gone missing?"

Christine filled the mug with water and set it on the table. "Yes. I believe I told you about it. The Automation teacher hasn't been heard from in three weeks."

Gérard shrugged, accepting that he'd forgotten yet another thing she'd told him. "Well, apparently, the police are interviewing the kids and the parents, and since I had an hour to kill this afternoon, I called them."

"How did that go?" Christine set the casserole on the trivet and took her seat.

"They asked if we'd seen anything on the Wednesday he'd gone missing. Also where we'd been. Hah! As if one of the parents would take off with the Automation teacher!"

"Quite."

"Anyway, I told them I'd been at work and that you'd been busy all day. I remember it quite clearly. You'd been really busy that Wednesday. Vacuuming, laundry, gardening. That's the day you turned the well into a compost!"

Christine filled her husband's plate, then her own. "Was it? I can hardly tell one Wednesday from the next."

"Oh, yes. I remember. You'd had so much to do, it wasn't even all done when I got home. Vacuum out, clothes on the bed, gardening tools by the door." He gave Christine a big, bright smile. "I don't know how you do it all."

Christine smiled back at her husband. "You'd be surprised what a mother can do once she sets her mind to it."

COLD BLUE ETERNITY

ONE

THE ENTIRE VILLAGE is going crazy.

It might not seem all that surprising at first glance. Our tiny village is perched on the mountainside of one of the higher Alps, in a valley so tight and closed-in we only get direct sunlight for a few hours in winter and very little cool air in summer, despite the altitude. The tree line snakes past less than one hundred meters below the first houses, giving us a couple of hundred meters of barren ground for us to latch onto, before the glacier eats up the rest of the valley.

The tourists are always in awe of the glacier looming above us at all times. Us locals don't really see it anymore. It's just there. A constant cold and blue presence creeping down the valley, lying in wait for the unwary.

The gray stone village buildings stand neatly aligned in five almost parallel horizontal lines, following the main—and only—road as it slings its way back and forth up the steep mountain.

There are, of course, nothing but hairpin bends on our road, but one of them is *the* hairpin bend; the one in the middle, the one going the farthest out, the biggest one. The one where the tourists get nervous in their buses as the front of the vehicle hangs over nothing but empty space in order to be able to make the turn.

This is where the crazy hits a new high.

The change has been subtle, creeping up on us over the span of several summers, swelling in time with the waves of heat creeping up the valley, apparently coming all the way from Africa, full of desert sand.

It's not exactly like a wave, though—the crazy never goes back out. Every time the temperature spikes, the crazy increases. When the temperature goes down to a somewhat normal level, the crazy stabilizes.

It doesn't decrease.

Our community is a small one. The village has more hotels and rental apartments than permanent residences. There are well over two thousand beds total but only three hundred of those are occupied by the same people every night, year round.

We welcome all the tourists, love to show them our world, make sure they have a good time while they're visiting so they'll learn to love the place like we do—but they're not part of our community. They're not *us*. They're *them*.

In winter, when the Alps around us are stark, snow-capped peaks contrasting beautifully against the azure sky and our breaths come out in clear, white puffs, *they* go skiing, and snowboarding, and snowshoeing, and sledding, while *we* prepare their food, make their beds, keep the roads clear of snow, watch and secure against avalanches, take the daredevils to the safe places for off-piste skiing, and guide group after group up to walk on the glacier.

In summer, when the air is hot and humid and heavy and the peaks seem like mirages shimmering in front of a blueish haze of a sky, and hydrating becomes the number one priority for locals and tourists alike, *they* go hiking, and biking, and spelunking, and tree climbing, while *we* still prepare their food and make their beds, keep the trails free of fallen trees, secure the tree-climbing itinerary—and guide group after group up to walk on the glacier.

It's thanks to the tourists that we can continue living in our village. They're our sole source of income.

But *they* will never be one of *us*.

And now the crazy is also affecting the tourists.

The first case that I can remember was ten years ago. Old Madame Teysseyre, who ran the oldest *boulangerie* in the village, started poisoning her cookies. Not the bread, not the cakes, not the various desserts. Just the cookies. An entire busload of German tourists got sick one weekend, which was enough to get the police involved. Some others had gotten sick before that but they mostly put it down to catching a random stomach bug and didn't inform anyone local of the fact that they spent twenty-four hours bent over the toilet bowl.

The police did their investigation, discovered the Germans had all bought Madame Teysseyre's cookies, bought the latest batch from the boulangerie and had them tested—and shut the place down the next day.

Madame Teysseyre never stopped claiming her innocence and got away with a hefty fine and was banned from running a business involving food ever again.

The really weird thing? I visited Madame Teysseyre a couple of years later and when she asked me if I wanted a snack with my coffee, I asked for cookies. Don't ask me why, my mouth talked without checking in with my brain.

At first, I was afraid she'd take offense but the word didn't seem to have any effect on her—except to light up her face in a huge smile at the idea of baking cookies for me.

Just to play it safe, I went with her to the kitchen and watched everything she put into those cookies. Flour, butter, sugar, chocolate chips, eggs…everything went fine until she opened a small jar standing inconspicuously in the corner and sprinkled white powder into the dough.

"What's that?" I asked.

"Poison," she answered lightly in a tone I'd have used to say "sugar," and went on to spoon the dough out on a baking sheet.

When I asked her about it again two minutes later, she had no idea what I was talking about.

Needless to say, I never ate the cookies.

Since then, numerous villagers have had similar cases of what I can only name temporary insanity. Like Madame Teysseyre with her cookies, they all had *one* situation where they became someone else, doing hurtful things, getting themselves or others in trouble—and not remembering a thing about it mere minutes later.

Lionel Manson tried to rob the bank every single time he went there. He seemed to really want to do it with a gun, except he didn't have one, so once he made one out of wood—not an actual gun, just a piece of wood with the general shape—and once he attempted to go in with a red and blue plastic play gun he'd bought in the toy store. Nobody, the police included, thought he was a real threat, but we couldn't let him keep scaring the tourists with his "hold-ups" so the solution became making sure he never set foot in the bank. His friends and family went for him when needed, and we haven't had a hold-up since.

Margot Santos became violent with her husband every time he tried to cook. She kicked his knee out of joint when he was trying to cook some pasta at three in the morning after a night out with the guys, gave him a solid shiner when he prepared a sandwich for their son's school picnic one morning, and pushed him in the pool when he tried to help out at the neighborhood barbecue at the end of summer. Margot didn't remember a thing, of course, and we all started to see a pattern. It was decided that it would be best for everyone if Margot's husband never attempted to cook while she was near ever again, and they've been back to the perfectly happy couple ever since.

I've been documenting the crazy since Lionel. The new cases usually come in spring and summer. One appeared mid-winter but I'm convinced that it arrived earlier and just didn't get triggered before the snow settled. After all, Jean-Pierre's crazy was to push people into the half-frozen lake after dark. I did a test with him in August, and he showed no signs of wanting to push me in—the freezing temperature of the water seemed to be part of his trigger.

No more walks by the lake in winter for Jean-Pierre.

I keep documenting new cases—I have a total of fifty-four—but no crazy ever seems to go away. With the people who have "safe" cases, I do tests from time to time, hoping the crazy will wear off, or go away completely.

But Madame Teysseyre's cookies still have poison in them, Lionel still wants to rob the bank, and Jean-Pierre still pushes me in the lake if it's cold enough. Margot will just have to stay untested.

And now…three tourists have caught the crazy.

TWO

THREE YOUNG MEN in their early twenties were arrested last night for assault and attempted rape of a young woman. On first sight, it might not be obvious that it's a case of the crazies but once I look closer it becomes obvious.

First reason: the victim and the three men are all part of a group from Bordeaux who is supposed to stay for two weeks. They're going hiking, tree climbing, and spelunking. From what I've seen—and I've had the chance to observe them from up close when I took them to the glacier two days ago—they're a fairly close-knit group, with several couples already formed and everybody telling each other they have to keep in touch once they get back home. That isn't just talk, these people are really planning on staying friends.

The victim and one of the three men were one of the newly formed couples. When questioned by the police, the woman told them her boyfriend was "unrecognizable" and that she got the feeling he had no idea who she was. The young men, of course, remembered nothing of the entire incident.

The police are blaming alcohol.

Everybody local blames the crazy—but none of us is about to say so.

I'm in the back office of my family's business—we specialize in taking people up to the glacier, different paths and difficulty levels depending on the price and the experience of our clients—logging the latest case of crazy in my logbook.

I write down every detail I know, not knowing yet what might be important. What was the trigger? What is *the action*? Is it actual rape and the young men were interrupted by something throwing the spell off them, or will it always stay at *attempted* rape? From what I understood from the victim, she was completely at their mercy with half her clothes off when they suddenly stopped, let her go, and took off down the street as if nothing had happened.

I write the words "Three men working in tandem" and underline them three times. They were definitely working together and none of them seem to have any memory of what they did to their friend. Somehow they have been taken by the same crazy.

Why? Were they in the same place when it happened? If Lionel had been with someone when he was hit, would we have had three bank robbers instead of one? Or did they somehow get hit by three crazies at the same time?

Which would be new…and very worrisome.

"What are you growling about?" My grandmother's voice comes from the front desk. "We won't be getting any new clients if they hear their guide talking to herself."

I close my notebook and join Mamie at the desk. She shouldn't be here, working, at the age of eighty-two, but nobody's managed to get her to stay at home. "My entire life has evolved around that glacier in one way or another," she always says. "And you want me to just stop because *you* think I'm old? I think not."

There isn't much we can say to that and hope to stay alive. At least she's no longer taking tourists up to the glacier and seems satisfied with manning the desk and telling stories to whoever is willing to listen.

"I thought we agreed your sister would take care of the finances," Mamie says as I perch on the edge of her desk. "Let her pretty little head worry about it."

The glint in her eyes makes me smile—my sister *hates* it when someone uses that expression, so Mamie does so at every opportunity.

"I wasn't working on the numbers," I tell her. "Believe me, I'm more than happy to leave that with Joséphine." She decided to study the stuff, after all. Better her than me. "I was thinking about those young men who were arrested last night."

"What happened this time? Couldn't hold their liquor?"

I shake my head. "Apparently none of them were drunk. You remember that group from Bordeaux from three days ago? I took them into the grotto."

"Of course I remember. I remember every single face that comes through here. Maybe you're the one going senile, if you forget something so important about your own grandmother."

I lean in to give her a quick kiss on the cheek. "I know you have the memory of an elephant, Mamie." Before she can get offended again, I plow on. "Three of the men from the group attempted to rape one of the women when she was walking back to their hotel last night."

Mamie straightens in her chair and her sharp eyes stare straight into mine. "Attempted, you say? They were interrupted?"

"No, that's just it. From what Fred told me, they left the bar shortly after the woman, with the intention of making sure she'd get home safely. She had refused their offer to accompany her, saying it was just five hundred meters down the road, but they worried anyway. So they followed her. And attacked her just as she reached the hairpin bend." I shake my head at the illogic of it all.

I'm about to continue when I realize Mamie's breathing has turned shallow and her face pale.

"The hairpin bend?" she whispers.

"Yes. What is it, Mamie? What's wrong?"

"She was attacked *at the hairpin bend*?"

"Yes." I kneel down on the floor next to her chair, taking her shaking hand in mine. "Has this happened before, Mamie?" Could the crazies somehow be moving between people now? How come I'd never heard of it?

"I was twenty-two," Mamie says in a weak voice, her gaze distant. "I'd stayed a little too late at your grandfather's place and was worried what my parents would say when I got home. I wasn't paying much attention to my surroundings. They came out of nowhere."

"You?" I grab her shoulders and pull her to me for a quick hug before pulling away just far enough to see her face. "This happened to you? Who was it? Were they caught? Who was it? I'm going to go kick their asses myself."

She chuckles faintly at this. "That's so sweet of you, Emma. I have no doubt you would teach them a lesson. But they're long dead, all three of them. And I'm fine, thanks to your grandfather."

"What did he do?"

"That's the night I learned that he always followed me home when I'd been visiting—but from a distance, so as not to hurt my pride. He caught them before they could go through with the act they were planning but not before they threw me to the ground and got most of my clothes off."

"Please tell me they paid for what they did, Mamie."

Her gaze drops to our joined hands. She gives me a squeeze. "I asked him not to tell the police," she whispers. "It would mean explaining why I was out there so late all by myself and was afraid this would mean my parents opposing us getting married. I did not want to risk it."

"So they walked?"

"Well, not quite." A corner of her mouth ticks up in a smile. "Your grandfather, finding himself at one against three, didn't hesitate to get creative. He hit two of them on the head with large stones before they realized he was even there. One of those was never the same again and walked himself off a cliff a couple of years later. The other suffered severe headaches for the rest of his life."

"And the third one?"

"Well." She pats my hand. "The third put up more of a fight and your grandfather ended up pushing him over the railing at the end of the hairpin."

My eyebrows shoot up. "That's a four-hundred-meter drop."

"Quite so."

"And Papy didn't get in trouble for that?"

Mamie shrugs her shoulders. "Who was to say he was ever there? The talk around town was that the three friends had gotten into a drunken fight that night. Me and your grandfather were never mentioned."

We sit in silence as I take it all in.

My grandmother was assaulted in her youth. And now the exact same scenario happened, except the men stopped by themselves even though there was nobody to fight them this time.

"I wouldn't worry too much about it," my grandmother says and gives my head a pat. "Like my mother used to say: the glacier will take care of them."

"Huh? What does the glacier have to do with anything? Papy didn't bury them up there, did he?"

Mamie howls with laughter. "The ideas you have, Emma. Do you not know the story?"

I shake my head.

"Legend has it the glacier is a kind of purgatory. It holds the souls of the damned prisoners until they have purged their sins. Because the glacier is eternal, see? They'll never get out." She waves a hand in the air and turns back to the computer. Back to work, walk down memory lane finished. "It's just a local legend, *chérie*. Something to help us feel better about people like those men not getting justice served in real life."

As my grandmother goes back to work, I just stand there, my mind whirring.

Souls stuck in the glacier as purgatory for all eternity. Because a glacier is, by definition, constant.

Except is isn't anymore.

Little by little, heat wave by heat wave, it's melting.

THREE

The next morning, I find myself knocking at the door of my main competitor. Anne Soumare is in her mid-fifties, has spent all of her life in the village except for the years she studied to be a teacher—and even then she didn't go farther than Lyon—used to *be* the teacher at our school when we still had a school, and now runs one of the three companies that offers outings up to the glacier. Where we specialize in going the farthest—both farthest up on the glacier and farthest inside it—she knows all the history. Her trips only require solid footwear and adequate clothing depending on the weather and time of year, while our most taxing outings have minimum physical requirements that often have us refusing service to overly optimistic tourists.

"Emma, what brings you here?" she asks me when she opens her office door. I had a feeling she'd be there despite the sign on the door saying it's closed. Her graying short hair is neatly coiffed as always, her brown eyes framed by black hipster glasses that she's been wearing for longer than they've been in fashion. She's wearing jeans, a black t-shirt, and hiking boots—what qualifies as work uniform around here.

"I have some history questions for you," I say, running a hand through my hair. I didn't bother to brush it this morning, just shoved it all into a messy ponytail. "Well, maybe more of a myth question."

"Thinking of expanding on your repertoire? Adding in some local history?"

I laugh along with her. We might say we're competitors but there are enough tourists to share and the reality is honestly closer to us being coworkers. "Nobody can tell a story like you, Anne. I wouldn't dream to even attempt it. This is for…something else."

She invites me in for a cup of coffee and we settle into the couch in her living area—the one in front of the floor-to-ceiling windows giving a panoramic view of the valley below us.

"Why don't any of us set up for views of the glacier?" I muse. "That's what most people are here for, right? Why do we give them a view of the exit while they wait?"

"That's your history question?" Anne smiles into her cup.

I snort. "No." Taking a sip of my coffee, I gather my thoughts. "My grandmother told me about a legend saying that the souls of the damned get imprisoned in the glacier. A purgatory of sorts. Have you heard this before?"

"Of course I have." Anne waves a hand. "You haven't? It's a favorite with the Saturday bingo crowd. But I guess you don't hang out there much, do you?"

Well, no. I'm more likely to be at one of the bars. With the rest of the below-eighty crowd. "You go to bingo night?"

Anne shrugs with a fond smile. "From time to time. It's a great place to learn old history and anecdotes to use for my guided trips, so… Now that almost all the young people take off to conquer the world and hardly any of them come back—present company excluded—I feel like it's important to document all the histories that were only transmitted from one generation to the next. The people who have lived here all their lives aren't going to share that stuff with outsiders."

True enough. Arguing with the older crowd that the tourists bring in money and are the only reason our village is still able to survive is a lost cause. They don't like the noise, the new constructions, the litter, the traffic.

"So, the glacier?" I prod.

Anne pulls her feet under herself on the couch and snuggles in with her coffee. "The legend is just what you said. The souls of sinners end up in the glacier to pay their way to redemption." She lifts one shoulder. "It's a closer threat than the usual burning in hell. Has more of an impact."

"Are there any stories of the people who should have ended up in the glacier if the legend was true?" I ask. "Surely, in a place this small, there can't be much of a history of violence?"

Anne studies me for a second. "You'd be surprised. The number of crimes committed in this village over the last century is *very* high compared to the number of inhabitants. I have two theories: either it's because we're so far from the nearest

Gendarmerie, or it's because the air is so thin, people go a little crazy at times."

"We're at two thousand meters. The air isn't *that* thin."

Anne sets her empty cup on a footstool next to the couch. "Then how do you explain how a sheep herder picks up a gun and decides to rob the bank? This was during the war and everybody knew the bank had close to no money anyway, and yet he thought it would be a good idea to steal his absent father's gun and kill the teller at the bank and walk out with forty francs."

A chill runs down my spine. "He robbed a bank with a gun? And *killed* someone?"

"What? Didn't your grandmother ever tell you about that?"

"What about someone hurting their spouse? Do you know if anything like that happened here?"

Anne's expression grows dark. "That wouldn't be particularly specific to this village. You'll find that type of story everywhere."

"How about hurting their spouse specifically when the spouse was cooking?"

Anne's eyebrows soar. "That *does* ring a bell. Hang on." She darts into her office and comes back with a notebook. She rifles through it. "Here! In 1912, Judith Lemaire killed her husband because he tried to fry some bacon and ended up setting fire to the kitchen. She doused the fire, then knocked the man over the head with a frying pan, killing him on the spot."

I sit there, mouth hanging open for several moments, taking in the craziness of that story—and the fact that there's a definite link with Margot's crazy. Her husband is apparently lucky to still be alive.

"Was Judith Lemaire ever convicted for the murder?" I ask.

Anne shakes her head. "She showed up in court with the frying pan and nobody dared stand up to her. They ruled it self-defense. The woman was built like a tank, apparently."

"What about the guy who robbed the bank? Surely they didn't rule that as self-defense?"

"They never caught him. Took off in the middle of the night with his forty francs and was never seen again." Anne puts a hand on my knee. "What's going on, Emma?"

"How many more of those sordid stories do you have in that notebook?"

"Quite a few."

"Show me."

FOUR

THERE HAVE BEEN even more cases of crazy than I thought. I just hadn't noticed the ones who played out their "scenario" only once, and got killed or jailed as a result. Quite a few of them were tourists—which is probably why they didn't register on my radar; I only watched for locals doing the same crazy stuff over and over. And figured aggressive behavior was normal in people who weren't *us*.

The only reason I noticed for the last three was because it hit three of them at once, and the fact that they attacked one of their friends made no sense.

Now, at seven o'clock on a Sunday morning, I'm on my way up the glacier, Anne in tow, to "investigate." I have no idea what we're supposed to find up here but it feels right going to the source to have a look around.

It's not like I can go up to Margot and just extract the spirit—or whatever the hell it is we're dealing with—of the woman who killed her husband for wanting to fry some bacon.

Anne might not bring her tourists on the most challenging trails but the woman herself is more than capable of keeping up with me. We both have our solid hiking boots, our ice picks and crampons in our backpacks, jackets with avalanche transceivers, and enough food and drink to survive at least two days.

The sun may be shining and most tourists wear only shorts and t-shirts—we've lived here long enough to know that the Alps can be dangerous.

And we're planning on going *into* the glacier.

The path up to the tunnel entrance is black with dirt and rocks. We're walking on several meters' worth of snow and ice but it doesn't show. In winter, the path will be white because of new snow but in summer we're down to the actual glacier and it's covered in years' worth of dirt and sand, not to mention the rocks coming up through the ice as the glacier slowly moves and evolves.

In this lower area of the glacier, the surroundings aren't much better. There's no doubt about the ground being covered in ice—it just happens to be dirty ice, with rivulets of sand and dirt running down the steep slopes on each side of the valley. The peaks on each side cut through the ice like stark, unforgiving giants.

Once my mind offers up the idea of the peaks being the guardians of the punished souls, I can't get it out of my head.

"You're failing at your job, though," I mumble at them.

When we enter the tunnel, Anne uses her key to open the box containing the light switches for the installation. We have over one hundred meters lighted up to make the visit safe and magical for our tourists.

"Maybe we only use our headlamps?" I say.

We share a look and Anne nods and closes the box without turning on any of the lights.

Modern installations and bright lights don't feel quite right when we're looking for tortured spirits.

I fasten my headlamp and grab a flashlight in one hand. Anne does the same and we walk down the tunnel.

"It's a lot more spooky with just a couple of moving lights, isn't it?" she says. The cone of light from her headlamp lights up the statue of a bear that Robert carved out of the ice last year, making it look like it's moving and about to attack us. The tunnel ahead of us is a big black rectangle framed by white snow.

"Maybe we should start offering haunted house tours as well," I say, laughing weakly.

We move quickly down the tunnel, the daylight fading completely behind us. From time to time there's a low groan from the glacier as the ice works and moves. The sounds aren't new to us and I'm used to explaining to my visitors that there's nothing to worry about, that the safety of the tunnel is checked at least once a week and that a glacier is in perpetual movement.

But in the dark, while searching for spirits…I could have done without the groaning.

We reach the end of the official tour, where the tunnel opens into a natural cave under the glacier. Here, the ice above us is sufficiently thin and transparent to let a cold, diffuse light through and illuminate the underground river making its way slowly down the valley under the ice. The ground is practically flat, covered in dark stones in all shapes and sizes. The sound of clear water sliding over rocks is enhanced by and echoed throughout the cavern.

The color blue permeates the entire space: almost white in the part of the glacier that's mostly compacted snow—the tunnel we came down through is cut through some of it; a beautiful turquoise that makes most tourists talk about the Caribbean where the glacier is all ice and not too thick; a darker blue going all the way to black where there's ice but no source of light. It's the most monochrome place I've ever known.

A barrier limits the zone accessible to the tourists to a tiny fraction of the cave, with several signs indicating in ten different languages that it's strictly forbidden to set foot past this point.

"You ever go farther in?" Anne asks.

"Of course," I reply, one hand on the wooden barrier but not yet climbing over. "But never with any of *them*. I sometimes go in to help map the movements of the ice." We take the safety of our tourists—and our own—very seriously and make sure that the movements of the ice won't put the structural soundness of the tunnel or the cavern in jeopardy.

We climb the barrier and make our way across the rocks, across the river, and toward the natural crack in the ice that the speleologists check out regularly. It's supposed to be the one going the farthest into the glacier. And it goes past a spot where the melting of the glacier is the most obvious.

"What are we actually looking for?" Anne says from right behind me as we start down the crack. It's no more than a meter wide but at least fifteen meters high, and several kilometers long. There's some light filtering through from above the ice but not enough to safely make our way forward, so we turn on both our headlamps and our flashlights.

"I'm not sure *looking* is the right word," I reply, my voice low. "*Feeling* for spirits might be closer to the right word."

"Great," Anne grumbles.

Time loses its meaning after a while but it must be close to an hour later when we arrive at the second river running under the glacier. This one is much larger and cannot easily be crossed on foot—we certainly won't be attempting it with the equipment we have today.

"This is where they say most of the snowmelt comes through," I explain to Anne. "The ceiling used to be just over the water but the last five to ten years it's been getting higher every summer. I think they measured it to ten meters at the beginning of the season."

"So, your theory is what? That since this is where the ice is melting the fastest, this is where the spirits are coming from?"

I just shrug. I'm no expert on spirits. But if they were supposedly stuck in the ice and now are released because of the melt… well, this would be the place they came from.

We spend the next two hours walking the space. We touch the ice, touch the water, listen to the groans of the ice and the howling of the wind, explore a few newly formed cracks in the ice.

I don't like the idea of giving up, but when the cold is getting so bad that my mind is offering up images of frostbite, I decide to call it a day. It was probably stupid coming here, anyway. What did I expect? A bunch of tortured spirits jumping out at me? And what would I have done if they did? Shine my light in their eyes and tell them begone?

"We'll try to check on the three guys from last night," Anne says as we walk back. "Maybe that will give us a clue."

FIVE

We don't make it to the three men currently under house-arrest in their hotel room. We don't get farther than the second hairpin turn on our way down the mountainside from the glacier.

Shoving my face into the passenger window as we take the first turn, I look down on the village several hundred meters below us, enjoying how small it looks in this huge valley. I like when things are put into perspective like this.

I remember one of the stories from Anne's notebook from the day before. "Hey, was this where that guy drove half his family off the mountain?"

Anne doesn't answer.

She's going into the hairpin turn a little fast.

Way too fast.

She's not braking.

"Anne! What are you doing?" I put my hand on the handbrake between us but refrain from pulling on it. It might slow us down somewhat but it will also make the car go into a spin, which is…not ideal on a narrow mountain road like this.

"Better to die here than on the front," Anne says in a voice not her own. Her eyes have a faraway look and her shoulders are pulled farther back than usual, making her look larger.

Before the last word is out of her mouth, she drives us straight into the crash barriers in the hairpin turn.

I register the seat belt biting into my torso.

The airbag deploying, slapping into me.

Blackness.

SIX

I DON'T THINK I'm out for long.

The radio is miraculously still working and it's still playing the same song as before the crash.

My head is ringing. My left boob is hurting like hell from being squished under the seat belt. My breath is short but at least I'm breathing. The airbag is already deflated.

The car hood is folded around the trunk of the large pine tree that's just behind the crash barriers—which we must have flattened on our way through.

Shaking, I turn my gaze to the right, to the three-hundred-meter drop mere meters from our car.

That's where the man I read about yesterday ended up. With his two teenaged sons in the car, he'd driven the car straight off the road at the turn, and into empty space. There hadn't been any crash barriers in 1915. The tree that saved us *might* have been a sapling back then, or possibly not even present.

"Won't go to the front," Anne mumbles. It's still not quite her voice and she's gripping the steering wheel so tightly that her knuckles are completely white. Her body is frozen in place but her eyes are moving, from the tree to the drop to the hood of the car.

She seems confused.

An idea takes hold. Figuring I don't have much time, I push away my doubts and play the role I suspect the spirit currently ruling Anne is expecting.

"It's okay, Dad," I say. "We didn't want to go to the front, either. Nobody ever came home alive, anyway. Might as well die here, close to home, where Mom can bury us and visit our graves."

No reaction from Anne. And it's definitely still *not* Anne.

"We don't blame you," I say, even though I'm guessing the boys in question would have preferred to try their luck on the front of a world war rather than crashing into the side of a mountain less than a kilometer from home. "We forgive you."

A tear forms in Anne's eye and she gulps.

The tear never falls.

I see the moment Anne comes back to her body. She blinks, the tear disappears.

Her eyes go wide in shock. "Did I almost kill both of us? How? I don't even remember. Did I fall asleep?"

I let out a breath I must have been holding since I realized we were going to crash. "You were possessed. It's okay, though. I think we got rid of the spirit. We, uh, should probably try to drive down that road one more time just to make sure it's really gone, though."

SEVEN

THE SECOND TIME down those hairpin turns, this time in my car, is the most stressful experience of my life. We make it down without a scratch, though.

The spirit is definitely gone.

"So we just need to forgive the spirits for their sins and they'll go?" Anne seems doubtful.

I nod. "I'm guessing it needs to be done while the spirit is in charge, though. So, you know, letting Lionel rob the bank, for example."

Anne's eyes widen. "And letting Margot's husband cook."

"Exactly."

The task includes a certain level of risk but we manage without any major mishaps.

Lionel gets to rob the bank with a toy gun, the teller—role-played by yours truly—forgiving him for killing her. When we try again the next day, Lionel is able to withdraw money, even though he has the plastic gun in his backpack.

Margot's husband has to play himself, since the trigger is clearly her spouse cooking—anybody else can cook around her without problem—but we make sure to remove all dangerous utensils and let him pretend to cook on a barbecue with no coals. Margot hits him over the head with a stuffed toy in the shape of a hammer, her husband forgives her—and the spirit is gone.

Madame Teysseyre gets to bake one last batch of poisoned cookies, which Anne and I pretend to eat before forgiving her. Then she makes her first batch *without* poison in over a decade.

The cookies are *delicious*.

We move through the list of known crazies and check them off one by one.

Then there's only the three tourists left, the ones who stand accused of attempted rape. The spirits of the men who attempted to rape my grandmother.

I'm not sure if I want to forgive those spirits.

Except I realize it's not up to me to decide. And for once, the person who *should* get to decide, is still alive. I explain the whole story to Mamie and her response is immediate.

"But of course we must forgive them. At the very least to release those *living* young men from the hold these spirits have on them. They can't be expected to walk around for the rest of their lives, at the risk of attacking young women whenever they find themselves in a hairpin turn!

"And honestly? I have nothing to forgive them for. Your grandfather made those boys pay quite the steep price back in the day. If they ended up in the glacier, it must be because their own conscience sent them there. It's a *good* thing if you can release them, Emma."

So I set myself up to be attacked. I have a lot of trouble convincing the police officer in charge but in the end he lets me do my roleplay—as long as he can watch from a distance.

I wait in the hairpin turn and the three men are told to walk toward me. They swear to everything between heaven and earth that they would *never* attack a woman, and how *stupid* did we think they were if we expected them to do it while the police was watching?

Still, they agree to make the walk.

And sure enough, the moment we cross paths in the turn, they jump me.

I don't put up a fight, even do my best to work with them on getting my clothes off. And I keep repeating, "I forgive you. You've already paid your price. I forgive you."

When I'm down to my bra and my pants are open, they suddenly stop.

This is how far the men came before my grandfather interrupted.

I continue the mantra of forgiveness—but I get the feeling I'm not getting through. They're just standing there like statues, staring into space.

"I forgive you." My grandmother's voice comes from down the road. She's approaching with the police officer, leaning on him for support.

The three men turn as one. Let out a relieved sigh.

And slump to the ground.

"Thank you, Mamie," I say as I put my clothes back on.

"I'm not the one who should be thanked," she replies. "The effort you've made on behalf of our small community is truly extraordinary."

Hands on hips, I turn to look up at the glacier just barely visible at the top of the valley as the sun sets behind us. The glacier that is melting, heat wave by heat wave. Releasing the tortured spirits of our past.

"Unfortunately, I think it's only the beginning."

SITTING DUCK

ONE

BRUNO TRUSTED KAREN. He'd follow her anywhere.

She was a small woman but had the strength of a grown man. She had delicate features, but never enhanced them with any makeup. She had street smarts and always spoke her mind. She took charge when it was needed and told Bruno what to do when he was lost.

As she had done tonight.

Whenever Bruno hesitated over what would be the right action in any given situation, he had Karen to guide him. It was such a relief.

Still, Bruno worried *a little* about how they were to get out of their current predicament.

He chewed off the last of the nail on his thumb and started in on the index finger. He'd finished his entire left hand in the car on the way home, and the right wasn't going to give up much of a fight.

"We can't just leave her out there," he said and spit the piece of nail out of the corner of his mouth. It landed on the lip of the kitchen counter.

Karen had been about to set a wooden cutting board on the counter but paused halfway to give Bruno a level stare.

Bruno brushed the nail to the floor.

Shaking her head, Karen dropped the cutting board with a clatter and placed a knife next to it. A large plastic bag filled with something green followed.

"Don't you worry your pretty little head with that," she said. "She ain't going nowhere."

"But…" Bruno searched for words while Karen pulled the green stuff out of the bag—spinach? Maybe. Bruno only ever bought the stuff pre-cut and frozen into cubes. The only reason he recognized it was that the package sported a picture of the real deal.

He shook his head to get his mind back on the issue at hand. "What if someone finds her?"

"Why would anyone find her?" Karen efficiently sorted through the mountain of green leaves, pulling off the stems and throwing them in a pile, and lumping the leaves into a roasting pan.

"Well… She's… What if…" Bruno's hands had no more luck explaining his points than his mouth did.

"Ain't nobody going to force open the trunk of our car," Karen said as she dumped the stems in the trash under the sink. "We've lived here for three years without ever locking the bloody doors. Nobody never stole nothing, even the stuff lying about in plain sight. Why would they start now?"

She put two casseroles on the stove, one filled with water, presumably for the fresh ravioli she placed next to it, and one in which she poured half a bottle of cream. While the cream heated, she brought a disk of blue cheese out of the fridge, at least 200 grams by the looks of it. The dish was going to be less healthy than Bruno first feared.

Bruno was down to the nub on his index finger and moved on to the next one. "Maybe someone's looking for her," he said. "People tend to look for dead people."

Karen shook her head, obviously finding Bruno ridiculous. "People look for missing loved ones." She paused the cheese cutting to point her knife in the direction of the car. "Ain't nobody loving that one. In fact, I'm betting nobody will say nothing about her not showing up for work for several days—they'll be too happy to get a reprieve."

She had a point. "Still," Bruno said. "We can't just keep her in the trunk of our car. What if a dog smells her or something?"

Between setting down her knife and dumping the cheese into the now boiling cream, Karen spared a glance at Bruno. "She's wrapped up in several layers of heavy duty contractor trash bags," she said, talking slowly, as if explaining something obvious to a child. "Also, it's bloody minus ten degrees outside, like it has been for two bloody weeks. She must be frozen solid by now and won't be giving off no smells that would make dogs tick."

Bruno shuddered at the mention of trash bags. He'd been relatively okay with handling a dead body. Watching said body being cut into pieces and shoved into plastic bags? Not so much. He'd just barely managed to avoid throwing up.

In fact… "You're not using the same knife, are you?"

Karen spared a glance at the knife while she spread the cooked ravioli over the spinach. "Why? I cleaned it. Used warm water and everything." Unbothered, she poured the cheese-and-cream sauce over the pasta, placed the casseroles in the sink, and pushed the dish into the oven.

"Dinner's ready in twenty."

TWO

Karen used the knife again while she was eating twenty minutes later. "No point in dirtying more dishes than necessary," she said when Bruno stared at the weapon.

Bruno had lost all semblance of an appetite, but when Karen pointed that blasted knife at him and said, "We have a lot to do tomorrow, eat up," he forced himself to finish his plate.

ಬ

The next morning, Bruno was startled awake by his alarm, so he must've slept a little. But it felt like he'd been awake all night, staring at the ceiling while Karen snored next to him. He always admired her *sang froid*, had been in awe of how she never let anyone mess with her or bully her around, and had done his best to emulate her in difficult situations since they started going out six months ago.

He'd thought that she could deal with anything.

He just hadn't realized that "dealing with" a colleague who was monumentally stupid, annoying, and stubborn, could mean killing her, chopping her into manageable bits, and figuring out a way of getting rid of the body.

"How are we getting rid of the body?" Bruno asked as he sipped his coffee while Karen prepared her breakfast. It was an absolute necessity for him to get some caffeine in his body, but it was out of the question to eat anything else.

Karen was using the bloody knife—again—to cut up and butter her baguette. She always carried that knife with her everywhere, but he couldn't remember seeing her actually use it before. Had he just not noticed? She was so comfortable with it.

As the thought crossed his mind, her hand slipped, and she nicked her palm.

"Would you look at that," she said. She held her hand out from her body so she wouldn't get blood on her clothes. Large drops splattered to the wooden kitchen floor.

Bruno jumped into action. "Here," he said and passed her a tissue.

"Thanks," Karen replied calmly, took it with her wounded hand, and bent down to mop up the blood on the floor.

"I…I meant for you to staunch the bleeding," Bruno said.

"Bleeding." Karen shook her head and huffed as if calling a steady stream of drops of blood "bleeding" was ridiculous.

The tissue wasn't really absorbing the blood, so she ended up rubbing the blood into the woodboards in a widening circle.

"Eh, why do I even bother." Karen straightened, dropped the bloody tissue in the trash, and picked a new one out of the dispenser, this time to use it as a bandage.

Before Bruno could figure out how to react, Karen moved on with her day as if nothing had happened. She put a large casserole on the stove, filled to the rim with water. She also started the water cooker while starting in on her baguette. From the top cupboard she eased out no less than four thermoses and lined them up on the kitchen counter.

Bruno hesitated, but couldn't stop himself from asking, "Thirsty?"

"We're going on a hike," Karen said around a full mouth. "Doin' some fishing."

"Fishing?" Bruno almost dropped his mug in surprise. "There's a dead body in the trunk of our car and you want to go fishing? Is this about having an alibi or something?"

Karen just stared at him while she chewed her bread. Bruno felt like an insect under a microscope, still alive but strapped to a cushion with a needle through his body.

When she finished chewing, she took a sip of coffee before answering Bruno. "You ain't telling nobody about our little excursion today, no, if that's what you're asking. If nobody knows when she actually disappeared, we won't need no specific alibi. We'll meet with lots of people over the next week or two, just in case."

Bruno wasn't following, but he didn't dare ask any more questions. He trusted her. He really did. She'd been nothing but a positive influence on him since they met, making him more confident and daring.

he'd been sitting on his hands for the past five minutes to try to warm them up.

Karen wore her winter clothing, too, but it must be of better quality than Bruno's, because she seemed unaffected by the below-zero temperature. As she bypassed other cars and trucks, she hummed what Bruno thought was *Je veux mourir sur scène* by Dalida. The dying part was accurate enough, but Sabrina had hardly been on stage when Karen had plunged her knife into the woman's heart.

Bruno tried reasoning in his head, channeling his inner Karen. What had she meant by fishing? Was it possible to find fish that would eat the dead body? Wouldn't he have known if that existed in the area?

And what kind of alibis would they come up with? What techniques did the police have to determine when somebody died? How precise could they be? He should have watched more police procedurals on Netflix.

It was certainly a godsend that Sabrina was going on vacation for two weeks. Although…

"Won't the airline be able to tell the police that Sabrina never got on a plane? They'll know she went missing before that date. When was her flight?"

Karen stopped humming and glanced in her blind spot before switching over to the left hand lane. "Don't you trust me, Bruno? I told you, I got this."

"Of course I trust you," Bruno said. "But you talked about having an alibi for the upcoming weeks. I just don't really understand why that's necessary. Wouldn't it be more important to have it all for right now? Up until the moment her flight leaves?"

Karen took a deep breath, as if searching for strength. She let it out in a low hiss. "Her flight's on Monday morning. What you gotta remember, Bruno, is that I know what I'm doing. And you're not great under stress. So just follow my lead, don't talk to no one, and we'll be fine."

Bruno nodded and huddled into the neck of his anorak. He did trust her, and it was freeing to know that she didn't expect him to take any responsibilities. He just had to follow orders.

They exited the highway and drove past Bagnères-de-Bigorre. Another thirty minutes on an increasingly narrow road, almost a mountain trail, and they reached Chiroulet, the tiny village marking the end of this particular road.

Karen parked her car in front of the church, got out, and opened the trunk.

Bruno came rushing back, looking in all directions, searching for witnesses. "You can't just open the trunk for all and sunder to see!"

"Seriously," Karen said, her voice clipped. "You gotta take it down a notch or ten." She gestured at the open trunk. "There ain't nothing to see."

She was right, of course. There were no body parts laying around in the trunk, open for anyone to see. The body parts were stuffed into four trash bags, and on top of those bags were two large backpacks and two pairs of snowshoes.

Right. Hiking.

Stomach heaving at the memory of all that blood, Bruno staggered backward a couple of steps as he tried, but failed, to put his backpack on as gracefully as Karen.

She was probably right. The backpack didn't weigh thirty kilos. Still, it must be pretty close to twenty, and several hours' worth of walking in deep snow wearing snowshoes would be a rough task for someone in as mediocre shape as Bruno, even without the backpack.

"Seriously, Karen," Bruno pleaded, "I'd do anything for you, you know that. But I'm not sure I can do this."

Slamming the trunk shut, Karen slapped Bruno on the shoulder. "Sure you can. I believe in you. Besides," she added as she took off toward a mountain track at the end of the road, "at this point, you ain't really got no choice. Off we go."

THREE

THREE HOURS LATER, Bruno regretted following Karen onto that track. He regretted not having gone to the police when Sabrina died. He regretted not reacting when Karen drew her knife.

He regretted being born.

His backpack weighed more than him, he was sure of it. His shoes had been soaked through for the last hour. He'd sweated through at least two layers of clothing and whenever he attempted a break to catch his breath, the wind blew right through him, making his whole body shiver with cold.

Karen was waiting for him some two hundred meters farther along the path. She seemed to have reached some sort of plateau.

In fact, she was emptying her backpack. Could they be at the lake?

Grabbing onto that little glimmer of hope with his entire being, Bruno forced his trembling legs to get moving. He followed Karen's footsteps exactly, setting his snowshoes in the yeti-like tracks hers had made. The snow was hard and crusty since there hadn't been any snowfall for well over a month, but it was still exhausting to stomp through.

Le Lac Bleu certainly carried its name well. Even covered in a thick layer of ice, it reflected the sky like a painter's perfect definition of the color blue. The Pyrenees used it to create a blue mirror image of their jagged teeth.

"See," Karen said as she arranged the four thermoses alongside the trash bags by her feet. "Told you you could do it."

Bruno didn't even have enough energy to reply. He just dropped his backpack where he stood and sat down on top of it.

The thought of sitting on Sabrina's dead body parts would have made him shudder, except he was already using all his energy to shake because of the cold wind sifting through his wet clothes.

Besides, he was too tired to care.

Karen slapped him on the back of the head. "Don't stop, idiot. You'll freeze to death. There's still work to be done."

Bruno shakily got to his feet, hissing in a deep breath when a gust of wind hit him square in the back.

"Wh—what do I need to do?" he asked.

"Bags out. Drag them out to the middle of the lake."

Bruno stared out at the large expanse of blue ice in front of him. "Out on the ice?"

Karen rolled her eyes. "Yes, out on the ice. It's on its deepest about two thirds of the way to our left." She pointed. "And halfway across to the other side. When you've brought your bags over, you can bring five rocks from the shore here. As big as you can carry."

Arms drawn around himself, Bruno stared at the trash bags as he halfheartedly bumped one of them with the tip of his boot. "We're dumping them in the lake?"

"Got it in one."

"Won't someone find her? This looks like a nice place to come for a hike in summer." The Pyrenees rose tall around them, forming an imposing and silent theater around the lake. To the north, they had an unimpeded view of the plains with Toulouse just barely visible on the horizon, if you knew where to look.

Karen put the thermoses into a smaller backpack which seemed to already contain some tools, then hefted one of the trash bags. "Le Lac Bleu is the deepest lake in the Pyrenees. Over a hundred meters where we're aiming at. We just make sure no bits float up to the surface and she won't never be found."

Bruno wasn't about to argue. He carried both his bags to the spot Karen indicated, happy for the workout to make him somewhat warm again, but unhappy about the added effort it demanded of his already exhausted body.

While he made two trips to bring the rocks Karen had asked for—ballast he supposed—Karen attacked the ice.

Bruno, who'd been looking forward to a cup of hot tea, had tears coming to his eyes when he saw her empty the last of the thermoses to melt the ice.

"You couldn't save at least a cup?" he asked, unable to keep the question in.

Karen shot him a quick glare. "Every drop saves me time with the drill. I'd have taken more if I'd had more thermoses. Stop being such a wuss."

Bruno's teeth were chattering so loud, his entire skull shook with the reverberations. "But I'm so c—cold," he whined.

"I know," Karen said.

She pulled a small drill out of her pack and set to work. The warm water had worked its charm, so it didn't take her long to cut down to the water, creating a multitude of small holes to achieve a circle about fifty centimeters across. Using a hook she'd also carried with her, she pulled the "lid" out and pushed it to the side.

"One rock per bag," she told Bruno. "No attaching on the outside. Open the bag, shove the rock in, and close it again."

Bruno tried to comply, he really did, but his fingers were unable to undo the knot on the trash bag.

"Seriously," Karen said as she hunkered down to do it for him. "You're worthless."

Bruno didn't care anymore. He just wanted to go home.

Karen made quick work of the bags, and one by one, dropped them unceremoniously into the hole. They all sank quickly, and Bruno watched them descend until they disappeared in the pure blackness below.

The lid fit right back into its original slot.

"Th—that w—will be v—v—visible," Bruno said, battling with his body to get it to cooperate.

Shrugging, Karen gathered her tools in her bag and started walking back to shore. "It'll freeze back in place. And there's snow coming over the next couple days—first snow in a month—so that'll cover it right up. Besides, it just looks like someone tried some fishing."

She kept talking about Martinique. She'd decided that was the destination Sabrina had kept yapping about during the party.

"That's where they drink rum, right?" she mused. "Beaches and booze. That's what she said, anyway. Was going to stay at some cheap hotel and sleep her way to better accommodations. If she can do it…" She hitched her backpack higher on her back as she skipped over a small boulder.

"Hey, Bruno? Me and Sabrina could look alike, right? Same height. Face has sort of the same shape. She's hella skinnier than me, but that doesn't show on a passport photo."

The next time Bruno caught up with her, she had changed the subject, and Bruno suspected his mind was playing tricks on him.

"Where do you go to get a wig done real quick? Those shops that sell Halloween costumes?"

FOUR

When Bruno finally spotted the Chiroulet church spire, his breath caught on a sob. Just a few hundred meters more, and he'd be in the car. He could remove all his clothes, put the heating on its maximum and stuff his toes on the dashboard.

Karen wouldn't like it, but Bruno had frankly had enough of Karen for today.

She was waiting for him at a spot where the trail turned into a forest track.

"Why don't you sit 'n wait here," she said, pointing at the trunk of a fallen oak. "I'll get the car and pick you up. You don't need to walk no more."

Bruno was seated on the trunk before he could even think about it. His body had accepted the invitation without checking with his brain. Then again, he was pretty sure his brain was slowing down, so maybe it wasn't such a bad idea.

"Great," Karen said and slapped Bruno on the shoulder. "See you in ten."

Despite his arched back, Bruno's sweater touched his back and he hissed in a shuddering breath.

Karen disappeared around the next bend and Bruno stayed immobile to minimize contact with his clothes.

He was so cold he wasn't even shivering anymore. He just sat there, feeling his body turning into ice at an alarming rate.

His brain decided to give one last kick: what guarantee did he have that Karen would come back for him?

His mind was about to go blank again, but he forced out a full-body shake and followed his original thought.

They hadn't been together all that long. Six months and living together for the past two weeks. Bruno had never met her family, nor any friends outside of their place of work. He didn't know anything about her past since he never asked any questions, and she never offered any information.

She knew everything about *him*, because she asked questions and he happily answered.

What if she just left him here? What would happen then?

Suddenly, he could see it. She'd find some other means of transport than their car—an Uber or hitchhiking—to get home to Toulouse for a hot meal and a long shower.

She'd go over to Sabrina's place, using the key they'd taken from her purse. Find her passport, tickets, and whatever else might be of value. She'd probably even pack a suitcase with Sabrina's things, to make it look right.

She'd figure out where to get a wig that would make her look like Sabrina.

And on Monday, she'd be on the flight for Martinique.

Would she be on the return flight? Probably not.

Which would make it look like Sabrina had disappeared in Martinique, not Toulouse.

Karen was the one who would be missing from Toulouse. Karen, whose blood was rubbed into their kitchen floor.

Whenever a woman was killed or went missing, the husband or boyfriend was always the prime suspect.

And where would Bruno be? Probably right here, frozen to death, looking like he'd just worked his ass off to get rid of his girlfriend's body.

It was tempting to just give up.

But Bruno was discovering a new source of energy, one he was wholly unfamiliar with.

Anger.

How dare she do this to him? He'd been nothing but adoring and nice to Karen, and this was how she repaid him?

He wouldn't have it.

Screaming in pain, he pushed up into a standing position. He wobbled but managed to steady himself.

The first house of the village couldn't be far. He'd made it up to the Lac Bleu and back, he could manage a couple hundred meters more.

He took the first step.

JUST DESSERTS
A Ghost Detective Short Story

ONE

We hear the screams as soon as the group exits the church.

"I think this one's for you, Robert," Clothilde says. She's sitting on top of her tombstone, the plainest slab of stone in the whole graveyard, with only her first name and a date of death. No birthday, no last name, no citation or drawings of angels. She's one of the greatest mysteries this place has, but she won't let me investigate. Every attempt I've made to ask her about her life has been rebuffed, sometimes nicely, sometimes not so much. She's been dead for twenty-five years, but she'll always be a teenager at heart.

Today she's wearing high-waisted jeans that stop just above her ankle and a white top that would have shown the straps of her bra if she'd been wearing one. Her dangling feet are covered in a pair of Converse, worn on the heel and one of the laces torn on her right foot. There's no telling the color—the dead only wear shades of gray.

We haven't had many new arrivals lately. The only people to die were old ladies with no reason to hang around after the funeral. When you've known for years that your time is almost up, you get your shit together and make sure there are no loose ends.

It's those of us who are taken by surprise who linger.

Of course, it's a good thing when someone goes straight to the afterlife. None of us wish suffering on another human being—or human ghost in this case—but it does get a little dull at times. There's only so much you can do to occupy your time when you're stuck within the confines of your cemetery, and it's the middle of winter so the number of visitors is at a minimum.

Today, though, we have a new arrival.

It's not easy coming to grips with being dead when you didn't expect it, didn't see it coming. It's a bit of a shock, to put it mildly.

Personally, I pounded on my casket for a week before realizing my fists didn't have any effect on the sturdy wood. Nor did they make any sound. My voice didn't echo like it should have.

Only when I calmed down—if I can really call it that—did I look around in the small space I occupied. And realize I was lying next to my own dead body.

I was laid out on white sheets, wearing my next best suit—the best one would be full of holes to match the ones on my body—my hands folded over my stomach and my expression relaxed in a way I'd never seen it before.

I'm not particularly bright, so it took me another day to accept the fact that I was dead and had apparently become a ghost.

That's when the coffin released me. The cemetery has been my home ever since.

As the funeral procession advances down the path from the church, my fellow ghosts gather next to me. We always wait for the new arrivals by the hole in the ground that will be their last resting place. We could have listened in at the church door and followed the procession, but whenever a ghost touches a human, there can be a form of interaction, and we don't want to freak out the bereaved any more than they already are.

So we observe the funerals from behind the priest, in the trees, from the top of the tombs, watch the coffin lowered into the ground, and settle in to wait to see if a new companion would join us.

There isn't really any doubt about this one being a keeper.

The screams are so loud it would have been impossible for us to hear each other speak. The banging on the coffin is strong, panicked, and unrelenting. I can't make out any words, only pure, unadulterated panic.

I want to go over and calm her down, tell her it's going to be okay.

But as long as she hasn't been released from the coffin, there's nothing I can do. She won't hear me.

And it's not going to be okay.

She's dead and she wasn't ready.

A lot of people have come to see her off. I'm guessing close to a hundred, which for a little town like this, is quite impressive. At the front are a couple in their forties who I'm going to assume are her parents. A couple of grandparents. Two boys who might be brothers. Behind them, a group I'm going to qualify as family. There's a large majority of blondes, with strong jaws and wide shoulders. The darker-haired or darker-skinned ones have probably married in.

Slightly to the side, a mass of young people. Probably early twenties, and about eighty percent female. The friends.

Some are crying, some seem to not understand what's going on. Probably the first time they're burying someone they know that's not a grandparent. One guy at the back leans close to the guy next to him to say something and receives an extremely stern and accusing stare in return. Not the time for a joke, my man.

I don't listen to what the priest says. It's all to soothe the family and friends and won't have any interesting information for me.

I'm studying the mourners.

More than half of all murders are done by a family member. Add in the large group of friends and the probability of the murderer being in view is pretty darn high.

Judging by the screams coming from the coffin, the probability of her being a murder victim is also pretty darn high.

I sidle over to eavesdrop on a whispered conversation on the family side of the group. I'm going to guess cousins. One blond woman in her twenties is speaking into the ear of a second even blonder one.

"I can't believe her mom made such a big deal out of keeping it hidden that she killed herself," she whispers. "I mean, come on, is her image really that important? She can't own up to her daughter taking her own life?"

I glance in direction of the coffin with a frown. Suicide?

"It's not just the image thing," the second woman whispers back. "Julie has always been very involved in the church. If it's suicide, her daughter can't be buried in the cemetery."

Which is exactly why we have so few suicides in here. *Could* a ghost be that panicked after waking up from her own suicide? Shouldn't the situation be a tad more expected?

People who are aware that they are in mortal danger don't usually need much time to accept what happened and move on. A couple of years ago, we had a soldier who was killed in Afghanistan. He only lingered long enough to say goodbye to his girlfriend then disappeared in a puff of smoke.

"Well," says the first one, "luckily, falling off a bridge with no witnesses isn't automatically ruled as a suicide. So here we are."

I move on, listening to people saying they don't understand how it's possible, the service was beautiful, the mother had made an excellent choice for the casket, the soccer game starts in an hour and a half, will they be able to watch it?

That last one is from the guy making the inappropriate comment or joke earlier, and it earns him the same look from his neighbor. "Seriously, Joss. I know this isn't your scene, but can you at least just shut up?"

Joss the jokester shuts up, clamping his lips shut as if he wishes they could be glued together. Despite the cold, a bead of sweat trickles down along his hairline, past his ear, and into his shirt.

If he's a talker, I'm guessing we'll see him again. Possibly for a confession.

As the casket is lowered into the ground, I stand next to the guy I'm assuming is the husband or boyfriend. He's part of the friend group, but also right next to the parents. His eyes are red and a sob escapes on each breath. Arms hanging limply by his sides, twitching now and then.

He seems genuinely upset.

At least he doesn't have to hear the screams.

TWO

SHE'S STILL SCREAMING when her talkative and inappropriate jokester friend drops by two days later.

I'm visiting Clothilde, like I usually do when I'm on the lookout for visitors. None of us understand how she managed to afford a place in this cemetery in the first place, what with the no name, no family, no mourners thing, but at least there's a certain "logic" to hers being the least popular spot, right next to the trash by the exit.

The main entrance is on the other side, by the church, but that's not where the interesting visitors come through.

"So how long do you think she'll keep this up?" Clothilde asks as she lounges on the ground, right on top of where her casket lies, six feet below. Her hands folded behind her head and her ankles crossed, she stares dreamily at the two or three clouds clotting the painfully blue winter sky.

"I don't know," I reply. "Not much we can do about it. She'll just have to get it out of her system." I'm sitting with my back against her tombstone, arms around my bent knees, and my chin on my knees. I'd put my hands over my ears if I thought it would do any good.

Even if we do this regularly, it still grates on the nerves to hear someone screaming in panic from waking up in a coffin for several days on end.

Clothilde grunts and blows at a fly zipping around her nose. The fly careens off course.

"We can't all be like you," I say. "Accepting that you're dead isn't easy for anyone."

"It is if you were as good as dead before."

Clothilde tends to make cryptic and worrisome comments like this. There's no point in asking her to elaborate, she'll only clam up. But I take note of everything. One day, maybe, I'll understand where she came from.

The rusty hinges of the iron grate squeal and the jokester comes through. He looks more at ease in a pair of jeans and a thick leather jacket than he did in a suit two days ago, but there are dark circles under his eyes and his hair doesn't look like it's seen shampoo or a comb since the funeral.

He looks left and right, making sure he's alone—it's half past ten on a Wednesday night, of course he's alone—before making a beeline for the new grave.

"I'm going to listen in," I say as I jump up and follow. "You coming?"

Clothilde sighs. "Guess so." She rolls into an upright position with more grace than a dancer. "It'll take my mind off the screaming. Maybe."

The jokester stands at the limit between grass and dirt, his tear-filled eyes on the wooden cross with "Florence Bernard" penciled in. Just as I reach him, he falls to his knees in the dirt and the air goes out of his lungs in a *whoosh*.

He leans forward, shoving his hands into the black earth. His position makes me think of praying Muslims. But he's not talking to a deity. He's talking to the girl who's still screaming, who still hasn't accepted her fate.

"I'm so sorry," he sobs. "It's all my fault. I'm so, so sorry."

Ah. A confession.

Although I don't have the satisfaction of having worked to find the culprit, at least I can tell the girl about it when she comes out. Perhaps it will be enough to allow her to move on immediately.

"I told them, Flo," the man continues, his face only millimeters from touching the dirt. "I told them who did it, but they didn't believe me. Two different police officers and they told me to take a hike. I didn't even make a joke!"

He sobs for a couple of minutes. His hands start to shake, probably from the biting cold, but he leaves them buried.

"This is why I always make the jokes, Flo. Nobody ever takes me seriously, so I might as well make it look like it's on purpose. You were the only one to ever really listen to me. And now you're dead because of that *bastard*!" A fist escapes the dirt and he slams it into the ground several times, gasps escaping as his body attempts to sob and breathe at the same time.

Okay, so maybe he's not the killer. It would be really helpful if he could give me a name, though. This is where being a ghost is really a drag—my suspects can't hear my questions.

"Everybody can see how much he loved her." He's quoting someone, complete with dirty fingers slashing quote marks in the air. "He'd never lay a hand on her. Can't you see how torn up he is? Of *course* he's torn up! He bloody killed you! He no longer has his golden goose!"

He sits back on his haunches and runs his hands through his hair. I wince in sympathy and hope he's planned on taking a shower soon.

I also wish he'd give me a *name*.

The man calms down. He pats the dirt back into place, as if having a perfectly smooth mound of dirt is Flo's greatest preoccupation at the moment.

"You shouldn't have done it," he says, his voice so low I can hardly hear him over his friend's screams. "We were *fine* as just friends. Worked out really well. You had your successful fiancé, the great job, the white picket fence in view. Everything you and your father had planned for."

He sits back on his heels. "Shouldn't have thrown it all away, Flo. I'd rather have had you for a friend than not have you at all."

Okay. Moving the fiancé up to the top of the list of suspects.

The friend—lover?—stays for over an hour, crying silently on the grave.

The screams from below continue.

THREE

It takes her ten days to come to terms with it. I'd say she's slow, but I was no better.

When the screams stop on the eighth day, I set up camp on top of her grave, right in front of the wooden cross, waiting for her to show her face. I'm a little leery of what I'll see.

I've seen quite a few horrors since I arrived in this cemetery, not to mention while I was alive, but it still affects me. If she died in the water, the question is how long it took before she was found. Some ghosts retain the form they had while they lived. A few of the senile ones are lucky enough to take a younger form of their bodies since it's all they can remember.

And some, the ones who stay dead for too long before becoming ghosts, walk around with cut up or bloated or maimed bodies, reminding everyone of their violent demise.

Florence, luckily, has retained the body from before she ended up in the river.

At sunset, her head breaks through the mound of dirt first, followed by two hands. She brings her arms up above her head, then lets them fall back down, watching how they aren't affected by the dirt.

She jerks when she sees me sitting on the ground in front of her but doesn't seem to tag me as a threat. "I'm a ghost," she says. It's a mixture of a question and a challenge, letting me decide if I want to answer or be scared.

"I know," I reply. "So am I."

She studies me closer, takes in the lack of color, the slight transparency that's more obvious during the day, my out-of-date fashion sense. She nods.

She waves her hands through the dirt again. "How come you're sitting on top of the ground and I'm stuck inside it? What am I even standing on? The coffin?" Her voice breaks on the last word.

"You're probably on the coffin, yes." I stand up and offer her a hand. "You can climb out on your own if you want, but I'm more than happy to help."

She eyes my hand, trying to decide if she can trust me.

"It's up to you to decide if you want things to be real to you or not. If you expect the dirt to have steps to help you get out, it will. If you expect it to let you pass through, it will. You'll get the hang of it pretty quickly."

A frown appearing on her too-young forehead, she studies the dirt as if it has personally offended her. Then she takes a step forward and up, as if she's walking up a set of stairs.

She's a quick study, this one.

She stands in front of me, looking around at our cemetery. I can hardly remember what I thought of it the first time I saw it. Now it's just my home, with the high stone walls cutting us off from the living world, the relatively small stone church with its seven bells, and the six hundred and seventy-seven graves. Some are mausoleums with pictures and statues of angels and seats for visitors, some simple tombstones with only a name on them.

She turns her sharp gaze on me. "Now what?"

I clear my throat and straighten my spine. Nobody gave me this job, nobody asked me to do it. I've decided to do it because I want to.

Because I think I have to.

I help the newcomers get settled, understand how things work. I help them find the closure they need to move on.

The closure I'm not sure I'll ever find for myself.

"The reason you're here as a ghost," I explain, "is that you have unfinished business. Once it's done, you can move on."

"Move on to where?"

I spread my hands wide. "That, I cannot say. I'm afraid I haven't made it that far myself yet. Hence my continued presence. I assume, though, that it is a better place. It is what we strive for."

She chews on her lip as she digests this. A speck of dirt that had stayed on her shoulder falls through her body and to the ground. She probably forgot that she's supposed to be covered in dirt after walking out of her grave.

"What kind of unfinished business?"

"Well." I clear my throat though there hasn't been a need to for a good thirty years. "It appears you were murdered. I'm guessing we're looking for the killer."

She doesn't appear surprised to hear she was murdered. "We?" she asks.

I crack a smile. "As you can see, there aren't that many things to do here. It would be my pleasure to help you out."

She nods. "So, we do what? Go haunt places?"

"Ah. I'm afraid we're very limited when it comes to haunting. We can't leave the cemetery grounds, you see. So we can only haunt whoever deigns to come visit us."

I see she's about to lash out. "I wouldn't worry overly much, my dear," I tell her. "You've only been in the ground for ten days and only one man has come to see you. There will be others." Possibly not before the tombstone is in place, though. People seem to prefer visiting a clean grave to a mound of dirt. Don't ask me why.

"Who came?" she asks, a first trace of vulnerability making an appearance. "Was it Joss?"

"I believe that was his name, yes," I tell her. I describe the man as best I can. "I got the feeling he was a good friend?"

Her clear eyes look toward the church with longing. "More than a friend. Or at least, that was the plan."

"Do you know who pushed you off that bridge?" I ask. "I assume you didn't jump?"

"Of course I didn't jump," she snaps. "I was finally going after what I wanted instead of what my father had planned for me. I was finally going to *live*." She takes a few deep breaths—a habit most of us keep even though we don't actually breathe anymore—before continuing in a calmer voice. "And no, I don't know who it was."

"What do you remember?"

She'd been on the bridge by herself, staring at the dark waters below, like she often did when she needed a time out. It was her spot, and everyone who was even remotely close to her knew it. She'd been listening to music, so she hadn't heard anyone approach. One minute she'd been listening to Beyoncé. The next she was flying through the air, seeing the water and the rocks below coming to meet her as she fell face first to her death.

"All right," I say. "So we don't know who the killer is. The good part is it means that might be all you need to be able to move on. Figure out who killed you, and we're done."

She studies me, skepticism clear on her youthful and pretty face. "What's in this for you? Why do you want to get me out of here? Am I stepping on your turf or something?"

I laugh, but it sounds hollow. "You're welcome to stay here with me as long as you like, Florence. I'd be happy for the company. But believe me when I say this: you do not want to stay here forever. It gets *very* boring. And the longer you wait, the more difficult it is to do what you have to do, and you risk ending up staying here forever."

She studies me, making me want to fidget. I can see the question in her eyes, but I'm grateful when she doesn't give it voice.

Yes, I suspect I'll be here forever. And yes, that scares me. But keeping busy assisting the others helps.

The hinges of the back gate squeak and I breathe a sigh of relief when Florence turns her focus toward the sound.

"Looks like we can start the work straight away, my friend," she says. "That's my fiancé."

FOUR

THE YOUNG MAN who'd stood at the limit between family and friends at the funeral gently closes the gate behind him, wincing at the resulting squeak. Hands shoved into the pockets of his fancy leather winter jacket, he approaches Flo's grave, his steps hesitant.

"I assume he can't see me?" Flo asks.

I shake my head.

"Hear? Feel?"

I tip my head from side to side. "Not like you're used to, no. But they do feel *something*." I wave a hand at the fiancé, who's almost at the mound of dirt. "Go ahead and experiment."

I'm guessing we'll need it if we want a confession out of him before he leaves the premises.

Flo sidles up to her fiancé's side. "Hey, Cédric." She cocks her head to look up at him.

"Hey, Flo."

Flo jumps a foot into the air and wide eyes meet mine. "You said he wouldn't hear me!"

I have to crack a smile. "He didn't," I assure her. "He's talking to your grave, that's all."

"I'm not sure why I came tonight." Cédric talks to the wooden cross, his hands still in his pockets and his shoulders drawn up so the collar of his jacket covers his ears. I don't know the man, but his voice feels flat, lifeless.

Flo steps in front of her fiancé, probably so it feels like he's looking at her. "What did you do, Cédric?"

I like this girl. She knows he can't really hear her, but my comment about them feeling something has her asking questions anyway. The thing is, I think it does help. They don't hear our actual words, but on some unconscious level, they must hear us, because two times out of three, they change the course of their monologue in the direction we want.

Cédric draws an uneven breath. "I swear I didn't know this was how it would end up. You must know I'd never do anything to hurt you."

"You didn't know how this would end up." Flo seems to taste the words in her mouth, trying them on to see if they fit. She turns to look at me. "That doesn't feel quite right if he pushed me off the bridge, does it?"

I shift my weight to my right foot and fold my arms across my chest. "Not really, no. But I'd like firmer proof."

She nods. "What did you do, Cédric?" she asks him again.

He shakes his head, tears filling his eyes. "I was just so hurt by what you did, Flo. After everything we'd built together, all the plans we'd laid. How could you just throw that away—for *Joss*?"

Flo raises a hand to his cheek—and her hand goes right through his head.

"You need to focus on the space he occupies," I tell her. "Expect to touch him, and you will." Sort of.

After shaking off a shiver, Flo tries again. This time, her hand caresses his cheek, though from the twitch in her fingers, I'm guessing she's freaked out by the lack of feeling.

"I'm so sorry I hurt you," Flo tells him. "But what we had was always more of a business agreement than a relationship. And I couldn't take it anymore."

"I guess I shouldn't be surprised," Cédric says. "Passion was never really our thing, was it?" He raises his eyes to the stars above us. "But *Joss*?"

Flo gives an annoyed sigh. "You're just going to have to get over that one, Cédric. But I am sorry for using you, even if I wasn't aware of doing it." She braces herself, then gives him a whole-body hug. Does it well, too. Not a single piece of her goes through the man.

I'd say he feels it. He visibly relaxes, his shoulders going down a fraction.

"What did you do, Cédric?" Flo lets her fiancé go, and steps back to stand in his line of sight again.

"Why'd you do it, Flo?" Cédric says.

Flo takes a step backward. "Why did I do what?"

A tear streaks down Cédric's face and disappears into his collar. "I get that your dad was probably pissed, but you're a strong girl. I mean, you *knew* he'd be unhappy about us breaking the engagement. Was that really enough to give up?" His shoulders slump and two more tears break free. "I just don't get it."

Flo's body is frozen to the spot. She turns her head just enough to look at me out of the corner of her eye. "What is he talking about?"

I remember the conversation between cousins at the funeral. "There's a chance people think you killed yourself."

"What!" Her head whips back and forth as she's trying to stare daggers at me and her fiancé both. "I would never do that!"

I step closer so she can look at both of us without giving herself the ghost equivalent of a whiplash. "I'm guessing this is the business you need to take care of before you can leave." I give her fiancé a once-over. "This man was at the top of my list of suspects, but for what we're seeing, I don't think he did it. Unless he's managed to convince himself you jumped of your own accord after he did the deed?"

Flo shakes her head. "Not his style."

Cédric falls to his knees, tears running freely now. He hangs his head as he sobs but doesn't seem to have the intention of talking any more.

"Let's look at this objectively," I say. "We know it's not the fiancé, and it's not the lover. Who else could it be? What could be the motive?"

Flo runs ran a hand through Cédric's hair, shivers and looks accusingly at her hand as if it is at fault for not giving her the usual feedback when she touches something.

"The motive is probably money," she says reluctantly. "I was planning on breaking it off with Cédric, but also getting out of the family business. I told him he could continue working with my dad, but I didn't want to do it anymore. I'm—I *was*—the face outward for our company. My dad thought, and rightly so, that having a young woman at the front of a business catering to mostly men would be good business. So if I'm no longer there, they will have to rework the entire business plan."

"Doesn't exactly point toward your competitors," I say. "If you were leaving anyway."

She shrugs. "Not many people knew, so maybe they just decided to make their move exactly when there was no need?"

I chew on my lip. "I guess it's possible. But I'm tempted to say it's someone from your side of things. Someone who wasn't happy about you leaving."

Flo points to the man sobbing at our feet. "He was the only one who knew. And Joss." Worry etches her forehead. "You're *sure* it wasn't Joss, right?"

"I'm sure."

She lets out a relieved sigh.

"Could either one of them have told anyone else?" I ask.

Flo pulls a hand through her hair as she thinks. "Joss didn't have anything to do with the business. Nor did the friends he hung out with. He's never even met my dad."

"So your dad is the one to run everything? The big boss?"

She nods.

"The one who has the most to lose if you left the company?"

Her eyes snap to mine. "He wouldn't."

"It does sound far-fetched," I agree. "But I didn't know the man. How was he usually in stressful situations? How did he manage his anger?"

Her lips twitch, and for a couple of seconds, she's about six years old and wearing a cute princess dress. Then she's back to her twenty-year-old self.

"What happened when you were a little girl?" I ask her gently. "When you were dressed up like a princess?"

Flo's breathing is shallow. Her eyes are distant, probably looking back at whatever happened that day.

"I ruined the car," she whispers. "I was dancing in circles on the terrace and stumbled. I knocked into a jar of paint that stood on the railing and it fell down on the car. Made a dent in the roof and he had to get a new paint job for the whole thing afterward."

I put a hand on her shoulder. She won't be able to feel it, but I'm hoping her memory can fill in when she has the visual. "What did he do to you?"

She squeezes her eyes shut. "He held me over the railing, yelling at me to look at what I'd done. Said he'd drop me, that maybe then I'd learn my lesson."

"Did he? Drop you?"

She shakes her head. "My mom came out of the kitchen and saw us. Had him put me down and yelled at him for an hour for putting me in danger like that."

"How do you think he'd react to learning you intended to leave him in the lurch?"

Flo takes a deep breath and lets it out slowly. She looks down at her fiancé, who's stopped crying but shows no sign of leaving. "I need to know if my dad knew," she says. "How can we find out?"

"There's a good chance he'll confess to it himself if he comes here by himself," I reply. "And they usually do, after a time. So we'd just have to wait." I meet her gaze. "The question is whether or not that will be enough for you to move on. Do you think *you* knowing will be enough, or do the people who are still alive have to know, too?"

She runs her hand through the hair of her wreck of a fiancé, without twitching this time. "They need to know," she whispers.

"That's what I figured," I say. "It means you have some work to do."

Flo straightens her back and sets her jaw. "Tell me what to do."

I point to the man at her feet. "You need to convince him to help you."

ଓ

"How LONG TO do you think this is going to take?" Clothilde asks from her perch. Where I usually try to respect the physical laws of the living, Clothilde doesn't care. She's standing on thin air to get a view of the parking lot over the wall.

I glance at the newly installed mausoleum over Flo's grave, with its brilliant gold letters and shiny surface. "Any day now."

The mom came by this morning, and Flo cried as many tears as her mom during the encounter. The dad was absent, though, and the mother promised he'd drop in soon.

He'll be here soon. The question is whether or not he'll have a tail.

"Ah," Clothilde says. "A Ferrari. Haven't seen it before. Might be our guy."

I rise from my seat and walk over to the main entrance, where Flo is waiting. "Your father?" I ask.

She nods.

Showtime.

FIVE

THE DAD TAKES his time getting out of the car. He walks to the passenger side to get his winter jacket and is careful with his suit at he slips it on. He strolls to the trunk, where he pulls out a bouquet of red roses.

"Mom bought them for him yesterday," Flo says. "She told me. Didn't want him to come empty-handed."

Fair enough. Not all men feel comfortable buying flowers.

The Ferrari is the only car in the parking lot. It might be happenstance, but if our suspicions are correct, he'd want to be alone today.

"A car just parked down the road toward the school," Clothilde informs me as she trots up to join us at the main entrance. "A blue Ford."

Flo's eyes light up. "That's Cédric! He listened!"

"Looks like it," Clothilde confirms. "I'll go meet him and see what I can do about those rusty hinges at the back door. But if he's no good at stealth, there isn't much I can do."

"Thank you," Flo says and squeezes the other girl's hand. I wouldn't go so far as to say they've become friends over the last week, but Clothilde seems invested in helping Flo get justice, and Flo knows to show her appreciation.

The dad looks around the parking lot as he approaches the main gate, and again when he's in the cemetery. Yup, definitely wanted to be alone. A Tuesday night at eleven is a good bet if that's what you want.

"Hey, Dad," Flo says as he passes us. "Long time, no see."

The dad stalks up the main path in direction of his daughter's grave. His expression is severe, not a tear in sight, his lips set in a thin line.

We follow in his wake, making sure to stay close enough to hear if he starts talking.

At the mausoleum, he sets the flowers down on the doorstep, then takes a step back. He takes his time in studying the little stone building set up in memory of his daughter but doesn't voice his thoughts about it. From his expression, I'd say he's not impressed.

Clothilde appears through the stone walls, hands raised and eyes wide. "Boo!" she says, then cackles a laugh. "Man, I wish that worked sometimes."

Flo's dad, of course, doesn't react at all.

Clothilde comes to stand with Flo and myself. "He climbed over the gate," she says, her voice impressed. "Tore open his pants and all but made it in without making a sound. He's hiding behind this horror, phone in hand." She points to the mausoleum.

"Guess it's my turn to play, then." Flo squares her shoulders and steps onto the first step of her new home, facing her father.

"Tell me, Dad," she says, her voice strong, "did someone tell you I was leaving?"

Her father grits his teeth and lets out a frustrated sigh. "Why did you have to do it?" he asks. "Why couldn't you stay on course? You were going to give up everything we'd worked for for *love*? Really? Give up a bright future with all the money and stability you could ever want, to go live with a guy who can't hold onto a job for more than six months?"

"Okay." Flo's eyes have lost some of their spark, but the determination is strong. "Someone told you. Guess it's not really important if it was Joss or Cédric, though I'm going to guess Cédric since I actually managed to convince him to follow you here." Joss had been by several times since she'd come out of the grave, and she'd talked to him about following her father, but to no effect.

"And now I even had to pay for *this*." Her dad kicks at the mausoleum, missing his daughter's ghost by mere millimeters.

"I'm sorry I'm always such a burden to you," Flo says. Her form flashes quickly to that of a much younger version of herself, then comes back to the version I know, anger flashing in her eyes. "At least you're rid of me now."

"At least I'm rid of you now," he echoes.

"Creepy," Clothilde whispers.

"Cédric came to me *crying*," the dad says, his own temper rising. "A grown man was crying in my lap because my daughter decided she didn't want him anymore. You take away everything we've worked for for *years*, and to top it all off, you break the one asset I could still use. What use is a man who starts *crying* over a *woman?*"

Clothilde takes off toward the back of the mausoleum. "I'm just going to check our little witness isn't going to do anything stupid until we have some definite proof."

"I can think of plenty of uses," Flo screams at him. "Cédric is a good man! He deserves a good life." She deflates a little and her voice lowers. "I couldn't give that to him. He might be sad right now, but I would have made him miserable in the long run."

"I was going to talk some sense into you," the dad says with a sneer. "Always standing on that bridge, wasting your time with God knows what. You'd just *sunk* my business, and there you were, *singing* and *shaking your ass* as if you were some ninny on TV who couldn't find anything more constructive to do with your time."

"I'm allowed to live my own life as I see fit!" Flo stands on her tiptoes, screaming into his face from no more than a centimeter away.

He flinches and takes a step back. He scans the cemetery but doesn't seem to see any of us standing around him, least of all his daughter right in front of him.

"Jeez," he says. "I'm even seeing things. See what you've brought me to? I'm staying up all night to work on finding your replacement, on finding a new marketing strategy. On figuring out what to do with that lousy fiancé of yours. And all because you can't bloody swim!" His voice rose throughout his speech and at the end he's screaming so loud, I'm surprised the neighbors don't come running.

"I can't swim?" Flo has taken a leaf out of Clothilde's book and is standing on thin air to get right into her father's face. "I can't swim? You know bloody well I can swim, since you insisted I learn when I was five! But I can't swim if my head's bashed in, Dad! I can't swim if I'm already dead! You did it, didn't you? You pushed me over the railing during one of your hissy fits, never thinking about the consequences of your actions!"

"Of course I did! You were just standing there, dancing, when everything was going to *shit*! You deserved to be thrown in! You deserved to pay the consequences! But you weren't supposed to die!"

Silence falls on the cemetery like a heavy brick.

"He just answered her question," Clothilde whispers as she pops her head around the mausoleum to meet my gaze.

"I know," I whisper back.

"Florence?" the dad asks, his voice shaky. He's looking right at her, not through her.

Flo's eyes are huge and her lips twitch as if she's about to start crying. "Daddy?"

The dad's eyes boggle, then roll to the back of his head. He falls to the ground like someone pressed his "off" button.

Cédric comes scrambling out from his hiding place. He takes in the flowers, the man sprawled on the ground. He's searching

SIX

WE STAND BY as the ambulance shows up and carts the father off on a gurney. While talking to the EMT, Cédric mentions what he'd overheard at Flo's grave and the police are called in. He shows them his recording.

"So it really wasn't a suicide, huh?" one of the officers says. "Good job on getting the evidence, kid."

After a while, even Joss shows up, and after a long discussion with Cédric where Flo listens in but I keep my distance, the two share a hug and leave together. There's not a dry eye in sight.

When there's only us ghosts left, and the cemetery is back to its usual silence, Flo approaches. She's still here, but I can see straight through her as she's becoming more translucent.

"Ready to leave?" I ask her.

"You think I'm done?" she asks. "How do I know if it's enough?"

I smile at her and lean in for a hug while it's still possible. As I step back, I wave a hand to indicate her body. "You're already on your way," I tell her.

She looks down at herself, at the fact that she can see through her legs, her torso, as if she's only just a memory of herself.

"Oh," she says in wonder. "Thank you." Her eyes are on mine as she disappears altogether.

I walk over to Clothilde's grave, where she's sitting, her legs dangling with her worn Converse going straight through the stone on every swing.

"Nice job, detective," she says. She makes a show of looking me over. "Still not enough?"

I sigh as I sit down on my own grave—a slight hump on the ground next to Clothilde's, without so much as a temporary cross to mark it. "I'm not sure it will ever be enough."

AUTHOR'S NOTE

THANK YOU FOR staying with me for these short mystery stories. I hope you enjoyed them! Feel free to leave a review or tell a friend, so the book can find more readers.

If you want more mysteries, I have a second short story collection coming out soon. It's called *A Thief in the Night*. There's also the *Ghost Detective* serieses, one with standalone short stories (you just read the first story), and one with a series of novels. And let's not forget the *Tolosa Mysteries*.

I also write in other genres. You can find a complete list in the next pages.

R.W. Wallace
www.rwwallace.com

Also by R.W. Wallace

Mystery

Ghost Detective Novels
Beyond the Grave
Unveiling the Past
Beneath the Surface
Piercing the Veil

Ghost Detective Shorts
Just Desserts
Lost Friends
Family Bonds
Common Ground
Till Death
Family History
Heritage
New Beginnings
Far From Home
Severed Ties
Eternal Bond
Harsh Expectations
Dull Expectations

Ghost Detective Collections
Unfinished Business, Vol 1

The Tolosa Mystery Series
The Red Brick Haze
The Red Brick Cellars
The Red Brick Basilica

Short Story Collections
Deep Dark Secrets
A Thief in the Night

Romance

French Office Romance Series
Flirting in Plain Sight
Hiding in Plain Sight

Standalone Novels
Love at First Flight

Holiday Stories

Collections
Heartwarming Holiday Tales

Short Stories
The Case of the Disappearing Gingerbread City
Crooks and Nannies

Young Adult Short Story Collections
Tales From the Trenches

Find all R.W. Wallace's books:

rwwallace.com/allbooks

www.ingramcontent.com/pod-product-compliance
Lightning Source LLC
LaVergne TN
LVHW041708060526
838201LV00043B/626